Rest Area

By Duane E. Coffill

For Mom, my number one reader, I love and miss you everyday…

Author's Note

This is a revised version of "Rest Area." The original version was published through a publisher who failed the original manuscript's expectations. I am proud of this revised edition and hope you enjoy it.

Thank you,

Duane E. Coffill.

Table of Contents

Chapter One

Ted Patterson, his wife, Terri, and their three kids, Shawn, Marla, and Lauri, were heading north towards Waterville. They went through the EZ Pass lane, which said, speed limit, 60MPH, DO NOT STOP.

Ted was forty-five, and Terri was forty. Their only son, Shawn, was ten. Their youngest daughter, Marla, was eight, and Lauri was fifteen. Ted had a bruise on the side of his right temple as he had fallen during moving and hit his head on the tarred driveway. He was examined and released from the local hospital and given pain meds. It was a start to their trip they didn't expect.

They were traveling from Boston, Mass. Ted was an Investment Banker for Moore & Moore Bank & Trust. He got a promotion and had to move to Waterville.

Terri was a Financial Director for Camden National Bank and worked remotely at times but would also be working in the office. The move was a perfect opportunity and closer for her.

Ted had a medium frame and a black dot on his right arm. Some people thought it was a mole, but it was a birthmark.

Terri groomed short, straight hair with greenish eyes. Lauri wore her short-brown hairstyle and had dark-brown eyes. Marla had long-medium length blonde hair with ocean eyes. Shawn was groomed with short light brown hair and had green eyes like his mother.

The family was in their SUV with four-wheel drive, and the color of the vehicle was silver. There was a secondary vehicle, a Black Ford Ranger, and Carmax would be delivering it to their new residence. This was for Ted, who would use it for work while Terri would drive the SUV. Beforehand, Ted had a Prius but sold it and used the money to buy the truck.

"Well, we just passed the Topsham exit. We're about another forty-five minutes or less from our new home." Ted said with an excited look as Terri took out the animal crackers, one of Ted's favorites, and fed them into Ted's mouth while having some herself.

Ted chuckled as Terri did, and some crackers spilled onto the seats and under them.

"CRAP! GET THEM!" He said loudly, almost with a panic tone, as Terri shook her head and told him, "RELAX!" She smiled, and he repeated it with a softer tone and slight smile. Then he saw her pick up the crackers and said, "Thank you for doing that," he sighed.

"You're welcome. Alright...a couple more," she said while feeding one cracker at a time, and he smiled and then thanked her. She quickly kissed him, and the younger kids in the back rolled their eyes and said, "That's gross!" Marla nodded while making the 'feeling sick.' look.

"I can't believe you got this promotion," Terri said while looking at Ted and then at the kids and asking them if they wanted animal crackers, which only Shawn obliged.

"Well, I've been with the bank for seven years, and getting this job was important. I was just surprised that the bank got us a house," he said while smiling and slightly shrugging his shoulders while driving, feeling excited.

"Are you ok?" Terri asked while looking on and feeding Ted more animal crackers, and he gently smiled and thanked her.

"Just excited, that's all." He replied with a smile.

They had to stop again for another pit stop after stopping three times on the way. They were approaching the Augusta rest area.

The kids grew anxious and had to use the restroom.

Ted drove the car off I-95 and into the rest area. Ted and Shawn quickly got out and walked to the men's restroom while Terri walked with the girls to the women's restroom. Ted stopped in his tracks after reading what was on the stalls and the walls within the restroom.

The men's bathroom was covered with ripped-up toilet paper, and there was graffiti everywhere like one stall had men suck cocks; call 555-5456, and you'll be satisfied within 30 minutes. Another stall had: *I love big cocks and hairy asses* written on it.

Ted grew a little nervous for Shawn, but he looked at Shawn, who ignored the writing and went to the stall.

Shawn went into the stall nearest to the urinals while Ted was in the next one, next to Shawn. Ted felt this restroom was used more for 'getting together' than the bathroom. Ted came to that conclusion also after seeing there were no stall doors. He grew very concerned for Shawn but knew he was next to him.

As Ted and Shawn were doing their business, an older guy came into the bathroom and stood at the urinal. He was tall, around six feet, slim, walked with a slight limp, and was in his early sixties. He looked over at the stalls before approaching the urinal nearest the stall.

He walked over to the stall next to Shawn, and then he whispered gently to Shawn said, "What's your name?" The older man asked sickly, as he didn't know a boy was in the stall and not a man.

Ted came out of the stall as Shawn did, and the older man ran out, realizing it was a boy, not the man he had anticipated. Ted didn't hear what the older man whispered to Shawn, but Shawn's reaction was what it was all about. He didn't understand what the old man meant, but he didn't say anything, and Ted and Shawn were at the sinks washing their hands, and Ted noticed in the urinal that the older man was at, white drops were dripping down from onto the floor, as had the older man gotten off.

Ted saw what happened and thought to himself, *what a sick fuck, knowing that Shawn and I were here; the sicko bastard gets off, and then he runs out; what a fucking sicko!* Shawn said nothing as Ted and Shawn quickly washed their hands. Ted and Shawn walked out. Ted's face was sickened with what he'd seen, and he couldn't believe what had happened.

Terri and the girls were still in the restroom as Ted and Shawn got back into the car and waited for the rest of the family to return.

"Shawn, did that old man say anything to you, I mean at all?" Ted asked with a concerned tone.

"No, Dad, he didn't say anything. He just went pee, and that was it." Shawn's tone was flat; somehow, Ted was trying to get the truth, but he didn't push it.

Twenty minutes had passed, and Ted and Shawn were asleep in the car due to the summer heat and waiting for so long. Terri and the girls were still in the women's bathroom, and there were no other cars after 'the creepy man' left. The woods behind the rest area and five picnic benches sat on a mowed lawn, but the paint had peeled away due to the weather exposure. The wooden benches were chipping away with some splinters on the edges. The rest area was small and very old. It had been built when the highway had been built. The roofing had been replaced numerous times along with the shingles, but overall, the rest area was in bad shape.

An hour had passed, and Ted woke up as Shawn was gone. Terri and the girls sat on one of the benches after seeing the boys asleep. It rained suddenly, and the raindrops awakened Ted as he heard them on the windshield. Ted briefly looked around and realized they were still in the bathroom and that he'd been asleep for an hour. Ted didn't know that Terri and the girls were sitting at one of the benches as it was on the side, and Ted could not see them. *Terri and the girls must have done some cleaning,* he thought with a slight smile.

Ted noticed that Shawn was not in the car with his him. *He must be with Terri and the girls.* Ted thought while deciding to get out and had to use the restroom again.

Ted ran into the men's restroom as he had to go. He urinated, washed his hands, and ran out, only to see Terri and the girls in the car, but no Shawn. Ted quickly ran into the women's bathroom.

Ted glanced around, seeing each stall was in immaculate condition.

Ted's emotions ran wild, as he was perturbed and the panic button had been pushed!

He moved back quickly, almost tripping over himself, Ted ran around to the back to see if they were behind the building, and there were no signs of him. His heart dropped slowly as he thought the worst; he yelled out for Shawn, "SHAWWWWWNNNN!" There was no response.

"Where is he?" He murmured.

Terri and the girls came around to know what was going on. The family noticed a couple of old wooden piles; maybe Shawn was playing hide and seek with his father. *This is no time for games, Shawn...where are you?* Ted thought while He and the family were checking the woodpiles.

"Oh, my God, someone took him," Terri said frantically. As the family continued the search and realized after hours of searching and calling the state police, they realized Shawn was gone! Someone had taken him!

Hours of searching for Shawn led to nowhere as the police, local volunteers, and we were looking for the child that disappeared, but what happened? Det. Mitchell was interviewing the parents to see if they had seen anyone else at the rest area, and both said no.

"Now, Mr. Patterson, where were you when your son disappeared?"

Det. Mitchell asked while looking and jotting in his notepad.

"Shawn and I had fallen asleep, and when I woke up, he was not there. I thought maybe he was with his mother and the girls. I used the restroom and saw her and the girls in the car, but he was not with them when I came out." Ted said.

"Now, was Shawn still in the car with you when you woke up?"

"No, he was gone," Ted said while holding Terri's hand.

"Now, Mr. Patterson, did you try to find your family before going to the restroom?" The detective asked with his eyebrow lifting a little.

"We fell asleep at the same time while Terri and the girls were gone," Ted said.

"You said you didn't see anyone else at the rest area while you got out of the car and went looking for the rest of your family. Is this correct, sir?"

"Yes," Ted said.

"Even sleeping in your car while your son was in the front seat with the doors unlocked is dangerous, sir." Det. Mitchell stated while pointing his finger gently at Ted with frustration.

"I didn't know this was gonna happen, sir. I just went..."

"That's all for now, Mr. Patterson." Det. Mitchell went to interview Terri as he asked Ted to give him a couple of minutes to interview his wife, as he was a little irritated. After two hours of questioning, checking the family's vehicle, the family was allowed to leave. Det. Mitchell thanked them, walked to his car, and requested help searching the rest area.

The family returned to their car and waited while the police searched the scene with the help of volunteers, who glanced at the family with concern and disbelief as they heard what had happened. Ted got out of the car while Terri remained in it with watery eyes, for the search for their son went on. Ted looked into the highway, thinking about how Shawn could have disappeared; *maybe someone took it while he was just around the corner or forced him out of the car while I was I was asleep, but why? Why take a child?*

Tears rolled down his flushed cheeks as he put his hand over his face, embracing the guilt and the possibility that his son would never be found.

Chapter Two

Ted and his family had finally arrived and brought in some of their clothes while the moving company arrived with their furnishings. Carmax arrived also and unloaded Ted's truck into the driveway. As this was going on, the police were still searching in Augusta and the surrounding areas. The family did their best to focus on the move, but Shawn's absence was disheartening.

Frustration was growing within Ted as he hoped they would find something, but there were no clues, and Ted was starting his new job within two days as he had to focus on that while the search for Shawn was going on.

The next day was the hardest for the family as time seemed to hurt more than help, knowing Shawn was still missing. Terri and Ted held each other throughout the day as it was the final moving day. They would have been done by now; unfortunately, the incident distracted them from the move.

Ted walked out onto the porch in the front yard as he watched cars driving slowly as motorists knew what was going on because the police had posted a report of the disappearance. This was done with the permission of Ted and Terri, as they figured it would help locate Shawn's whereabouts.

Ted and Terri's new home was on Silver Street in Waterville, Maine. The house was ten years old, and a couple occupied the home but left and moved to Denver, Colorado.

The house showcased four bedrooms and two bathrooms. It was on two acres of land and was white with teal trim. A patch of blueberries grew on the west side of the house and had been picked every summer by the former owners.

Terri swept the house inside as movers came and went with their furniture. This helped her deal with significant problems; while she was doing this. Ted was outside on the deck, having a beer, and the girls were unpacking boxes and putting things away. A box of Shawn's toys was in the corner by the sofa, with Shawn's name on it. Terri glanced over at it as tears started to stream down her flushed face.

"Are you ok, hun?" Ted asked while rubbing her shoulders.

"I'm doing fine." Terri responded quickly and firmly as tears rolled down her cheeks, and then tears rolled down Ted's cheeks. Ted walked around her, and they embraced. Four days passed, and Ted was enjoying his new job. To him, it was a nice distraction as the police continued to search for Shawn. Ted's employees supported their new manager and gave him cards, praying for his family and sending positive vibes. *This is a thoughtful gesture by my employees...I was not expecting all these kinds of things.* He thought while reading and smiling at the cards given to him at his desk.

The rest of the week went quickly as Terri had a small location at home for remote work, and she was also working her new job at the office. The girls were a month away from starting at their new school, and Ted was experiencing headaches. These were the same kind he had experienced as a kid but went away independently as he got older. He took some ibuprofen, and after a half hour, he started to feel better and focused on his work.

That evening, Ted came home and ate dinner, which was baked chicken with rice, and he thanked Terri and went to bed. Terri and the girls cleaned up the kitchen table. Afterward, Terri went upstairs and saw that Ted was already asleep. *I know he feels guilty, but this is unlike him...*Terri thought with a concerned look as this was the second time Ted had done this week.

Chapter Three

Finding your son is the possibility of finding Jimmy Hoffa's body. It will never happen.

Poor little parents. How they weren't watching their innocent little boy, Shawnee! Blood must pour to save ourselves from the inner society. Those who know shall remember the glory of my path, while others will cry in pain as they discover the truth! The stranger thought, walking past Denny's in Auburn after seeing on the news that Shawn Patterson was still missing. He thought this while smoking a cigar. The stranger remained in the shadows of Denny's while seeing someone he wanted to *meet.*

Gordy was 40 and overweight. He had never been married, but he had a few relationships, one with a girl and the rest with men.

He was living in Lewiston and worked at Live Bridge as a telemarketer and made good money based on his small salary plus commissions.

He'd been there for three years and liked it; even though they'd had financial trouble, they always made it through. Gordy sat in the famous diner in Auburn on 211 Court Street. He ordered the Grand Slam Breakfast, which was his favorite. He had a Coke with his meal and always asked for extra napkins as he was a sloppy eater. He ate at Denny's at least twice a week. Sometimes after work, depending on how he was feeling.

He sat on the right side, closer to the restroom. He also liked Denny's, besides the prices, but the *old diner* feel to it as there were a lot of seats, and Gordy loved how the restaurant always smelled like syrup.

Gordy was done eating after an hour and a half. This was typical of him as he paid the waitress and slowly got up from the red-leather seat while pulling up his tan pants and straightening out his white shirt with a red tie. He looked down and saw he had some syrup on his shirt. He didn't care. He was heading home and was going to shower.

Gordy drove a red 2015 black Versa Note. The car was a little snug to him, but he liked it. Gordy lived on Canal Street in Lewiston. After getting into the car, he looked at the diner and saw couples walking in. Sadness filled him, and Gordy drove off. The sadness of being alone and wanting a family was not going to *happen for me anytime soon.*

After crossing the bridge, which was 202, he made the right turn down into Canal Street. Headlights flashed him from behind, Gordy grew irritated as he was almost home, and the headlights kept flashing.

"Alright, fucka! I'm pulling over!" He said firmly. Gordy pulled his car over and got out while the car that was flashing him slowed quickly and parked two cars behind him.

Gordy was standing on the side, seeing someone getting out of their car and making their way to him. A nervous feeling started to grow within Gordy as he watched the driver make their way.

"Hey, you! Are you looking for something!?" Gordy stood with his slight numbness slivering down his back and yelled again.

"Hey, you, the person in the car behind me, are you looking for something?" Gordy asked with a firm tone, but deep down, he was scared shitless!

"Over here, buddy." The driver said firmly. Gordy watched as the driver slowly started to walk towards him, having a swagger in his walk. He could see that the driver was wearing a hat, but his face remained in the shadows.

Gordy started to walk backward, not knowing he had surpassed his car, and now his car was in front of him; he was heading towards the river. The stranger's footsteps were heavy, and he could hear him as if he were wearing cowboy boots.

"Are you some kind of...*Cowboy..?*" Gordy asked with a nervous chuckle.

The stranger was near Gordy. Gordy noticed that man was somewhat tall and had a slight southern accent. "Not quite, kid!" The stranger said firmly.

"I don't want any of this...I'm sorry," Gordy pleaded with the stranger.

"I know...I can *smell you* pissin' your pants!" The stranger said while his face remained hidden.

"Please don't hurt me...I'm overweight, and I don't have anyone...I want to go home!" Gordy was trying to back away, but he was scared stiff.

"I'm not gonna hurt 'ya...I'm gonna rip your FUCKIN' INSIDES OUT!" The stranger said with a firm and frightened tone as he lunged at Gordy, who tried to fight back, but then, his stomach and throat had been slit...he was bleeding to death.

Gordy fell to the pavement, trying to cry for help, but his vocal cords had been cut. The pain was immense. Gordy could feel his insides coming out, and he looked up at the stranger, who came into the light and wore a mask, and he said to Gordy... "Don't call me cowboy...call me Duke!" Duke said while watching Gordy trying to stay alive, and Gordy died. He was found hours later by passing cars, and something was carved across his chest.

Lewiston Police officers arrived, and one of them immediately grew sick. The other one called for an ambulance. Sgt James arrived on the scene shortly as he only lived two blocks away and heard on the scanner.

"Holy shit!" Sgt. James was shocked by what he saw as he looked over the entire body, and the officer that called for an ambulance wanted to show him the carving.

"Look at this, sir," he said while briefly lifting the victim's shirt and revealing what had been carved.

"Holy Mother of God...why would anyone carve **Duke** into a man's chest?" he asked with a disgusted look, and the officer with him nodded, and the other one returned and was feeling better.

"Are you ok?" He asked the sickened officer.

"I'm fine, sir."

"Alright, let's get some detectives over here and find out why did this happen? Sgt. James ordered the officer near him while getting his car and had to take a moment. His brown eyes glazed off and on at the crime scene. He was trembling a little, his combed hair was messy, but he pushed it back with his hands and returned to the crime scene.

Chapter Four

Sue Redding was running late to work as she was going 80 mph on the Maine Turnpike and passing cars as if they were in wheelchairs, but she didn't care; she would be late.

She knew she was doing wrong by running to work late because she had slept in and had been up late last night having drinks. When she got to work forty-five minutes later, her boss watched her as she was coming through the door, and she looked at the clock and knew Sue was late. Her boss looked at her quickly and Sue kept going to her desk.

Working for First Bank in Portland was like being in a circle cutthroat, where many employees bitched about each other and reported to their supervisors, hoping to get a promotion.

When she got to her desk, she glanced around to see if anyone else had noticed, but a lot knew of her being late. The only thing that kept her *somewhat* safe was that she had a good personality and did her job well.

She got on the computer and checked her email, checking the latest happenings at the bank. Sue was thirty-two and was married. She had no children as she wanted to focus on her career while her husband was a manager at the Scarborough Walmart in the deli section. Some coworkers called her 'Raggedy' Sue because she was a redhead; to some, it would be offensive, but she loved it!

The lights in the officer flickered at times due to the shoddy electrical work done by the last contractor. Sue would take incoming calls from customers who were clients. She would sometimes receive a call from potential customers who wanted to apply for a loan or a credit card. Her pay was substantial and more than what her husband was making.

Later that day, Sue was in the breakroom eating lunch while the TV was on. While eating leftover spaghetti, she watched the NBC news as they discussed finding a young man in Lewiston who was murdered.

*Oh my God...first a child, a missing, and now a murder...*Sue thought and decided to get back to work as the body bag of the victim was being carried away, and she was a little disgusted by the video.

Chapter Five

Ted was asleep, and he hadn't slept well in days, knowing his son was still missing, was tearing him apart. The house was still while the wind outside was slightly blowing.

The first day of work was stressful, dealing with family issues and trying to adjust to a new job. *These things were just too much to handle right now.* Ted thought while slowly walking the hallway and dealing with headaches.

It started to rain. Ted glanced through one of the living room windows, which oversaw his lawn and the road. He remembered family day trips to the Governor's restaurant in South Portland. That location has closed since then, while other locations have remained open. Ted remembered Shawn ordering a burger along with extra fries. *Shawn loved extra fries...every place we went...he always wanted extra fries.*

Tears rolled down Ted's tired face, and he took some pain meds and went back to sleep. After sleeping briefly, Ted got ready and went to the office. After arriving at work, he walked to his office with annoying lights and employees chatting away about work and their personal lives. He stared out the window as he was exhausted as he was up last night, dealing with a headache that's been nagging him since Shawn's disappearance. Staring at the computer screen was like poking needles in his eyes. He was able to complete his tasks and went home.

Ted wondered if there were any news regarding his son, but if he had heard nothing at work, he knew there was no new news. Upon arriving home, Terri looked lovely when Ted walked through the door, and he glanced at her, remembering how beautiful she was with their beautiful children.

"Wow, you look nice!" Ted said while scanning her from head to toe.

"You too, sir." She said with a smile that indicated she was inviting him to join her tonight. Knowing that Shawn was still missing, it's been a while since they have made love because of what is going on right now.

Ted and Terri lied in bed with their arms wrapped together, as they were cuddling, which many couples sometimes do, but not much, especially at night, lying in bed watching TV. Cuddling with each other, and then, they made love.

That night in the bedroom, Ted and Terri were asleep with their two daughters were also sleeping. The autumn air filled the house with chilliness and freshness. It was two in the morning, Friday, and the weekend was almost here. The girls wanted to do some shopping, but Ted and Terri weren't up for it, so they changed their minds as they knew nothing could be done.

That Saturday, they went to the Maine Mall and shopped for the day. Ted's headaches came and went. Ted was worried about him and encouraged him to see a doctor. He first declined to do so but eventually agreed.

They went to Best Buy, got food from Amato's in the Mall, and ate in the food court. They did some window shopping, which wasn't Ted's favorite thing. He sat on one of the benches while the ladies were in the Justice store. Ted watched other families walk by, some with young children and some with older children. His eyes got waterly, but he quickly wiped them away before anyone saw him. After shopping, they went to try on their newly bought clothing, while Ted decided to watch TV.

Sunday was crisp with the autumn air already here, even though it was only late September.

The phone ranged as Terri was reading her romance novel while Ted was outside with the girls; she got up from the sofa, went to the phone, and picked it up while still holding the book in her hand.

"Hello...Oh my God! No! No! Not my son!!!!" Tears were rolling down her cheeks after days of worrying and wondering how Shawn was doing...he was found dead.

"Ted!" She yelled outside, as her knees buckled to the shock, and he rushed to her, picked her up, and asked, "What happened!?" He asked with a concerned look.

"It's Shawn! They found him in a ditch!" She said with tears streaming down her face, and Ted gushed out in tears as they held each other, and the two daughters came over after seeing their parents crying, and then they knew what happened and that Shawn was not coming home.

Ted started to tell them the bad news while crying.

"Girls, Shawn's not coming home." He said while looking at them and seeing tears in their eyes. Terri, Ted, and their daughters held each other while dealing with the sad news. Terri started to explain to them as Shawn was in Heaven now, and she cried a horrible scream afterward.

The girls asked what had happened to Shawn. Ted and Terri looked at each other while they were both on their knees, and Terri said something.

"Well, girls, an awful person took him from us, and now...THAT SON OF A BITCH IS GONNA GET IT!" Terri said out loud as the girls understood, and Ted liked what Terri said. Ted and Terri were told they must go to the coroner and identify the body.

They had no babysitter, so the girls would have to go with them, as both Ted and Terri wanted to see the body. They got ready and made their way into the car, and left.

The radio played as they drove to Maine General Hospital in Augusta. Feelings of sadness, anger, and frustration filled the family's thoughts. They arrived at the hospital, checked in, and all four of them made their way down the hallway to the elevator to the basement.

The ride down on the elevator was tranquil as Ted and Terri were quiet, as the girls were hoping it was not Shawn.

Terri held Ted's right hand as they got off the elevator and were met with Det. Mitchell was the Maine State Detective they met at the rest area.

"Hello, Mr. and Mrs. Patterson. I'm sorry I didn't meet you upon your entering the hospital, I informed the staff to direct you, and I would meet you here." Det. Mitchell spoke softly, and Ted and Terri remembered him from the rest area as Det. Mitchell guided them.

"I would suggest having the girls remain in the hallway as this is something for them not to see. I would be glad to stay with them while you two go in?" Det. Mitchell offered, and Ted and Terri nodded and thanked him.

The coroner was inside the department as Ted and Terri entered. Ted and Terri signed a form to verify they had arrived and agreed to see the body.

Along with the coroner, Ted and Terri walked closer to the metallic table with a cloth sheet on the body. Ted and Terri glanced at the body while the coroner looked at them while slowly pulling down the sheet from head to toe.

"Oh, my God! No! I can't believe it. It's not Shawn!" Terri said with a joyful grin.

"It's not our Shawn. Thank God! Terri, it's not our baby. Oh, thank God, it's not Shawn, but who is it? Our baby is still alive." Ted said with colossal relief, and they embraced each other.

"So, this is not your child?" The coroner asked, confirming their acknowledgment.

"Yes, we both agree...it's not our Shawn!" Terri said with a slight smile as she and Ted looked back at the body; it was a boy, but his face and hair were different.

"Where was this child found?" Terri asked with a concerned tone.

The coroner covered up the body and quickly looked at the door and...

"This child was found in the woods, behind Farmer's Market in Sidney." He said while covering up the body. Ted and Terri asked more questions, but the coroner told them they had to leave.

Ted and Terri walked out into the hallway, and Det. Mitchell was their daughters, and the girls went up to their parents, and Terri said, "It's not Shawn." The girls embraced Terri. Ted and Det. Mitchell started talking.

"I'm partially glad that boy in there is not your child, Mr. Patterson."

"Me too, sir. What happened to that child in there?" Ted asked with a concerned look.

"I wish I could tell you more, sir, but I can't. I'm relieved that the boy in there is not your child, but other parents will have to face this harsh conclusion. Thank you for coming in." Det. Mitchell said while a pang of sadness was in his voice as he shook hands with Ted and Terri and smiled at the girls, and the Patterson family left to go home.

That night on the way home. Ted and Terri were silent, thinking about Shawn and how he was still alive and hoping he was okay and not harmed. The parents of that child that lay on the cold metallic table weren't so lucky, as the police contacted the next parents who reported a missing child just three days after Shawn disappeared.

It started to rain as Terri looked into the darkness as Ted was driving with their minds wandering off with endless questions and trying to find the answers for themselves, as to why would anyone harm a child? It was a dark question that fostered in their minds on the way home.

Chapter Six

Jack and Lilly Tate were traveling from Durham, passing Runaround Pond as they were traveling to Freeport, getting on I-95, and heading for Oakland to see Lilly's parents. They were driving a red Versa Note, perfect for gas as Lilly used it for work. Jack drove a black Ford Ranger with an extended cab.

Jack and Lilly got married two years ago, with both parents on the two sides disagreeing with the marriage based on the age difference. Jack was 37, and Lilly was 27, a ten-year difference.

Jack's parents said she was too young, while Lilly's parents said he was too old.

Jack and Lilly didn't care. They loved each other.

Lilly, a USM College graduate who majored in Business, worked at a business in Saco. Jack is a carpenter and is self-employed.

"I can't believe you talked me into going up to your parent's house," Jack said while driving, as Lilly looked at him, knowing that her parents never considered him *good enough* for her because of his job occupation and age.

"My parents don't hate you; they don't understand you; you know that." She said gently as she rubbed the back of his head while he was driving.

"You do know the truth. As long as we are together, I'll never get the acceptance my parents gave you, and you know that's the truth!" Jack said firmly, not to argue but to clarify his point.

"Your parents are great, Jack! I know they don't care about the age difference, but I'm not arguing about that! I can't help the way my parents are...It's just them!"

Lilly was a little frustrated as she stopped rubbing the back of his head and folded her arms while looking through the passenger window.

Five minutes had passed, and they were still not talking. They glanced at each other for a few seconds, and both were quiet.

"I don't want to fight with you, Lilly; it only matters that we're together, and that's it!" He said softly while putting his hand on hers, and she did the same.

"I know my parents aren't perfect; who is? But they will understand that you and I are married and will stay together for the rest of our lives, and that's all. Nothing they say or do will ever change that!" Lily said while reaching out and placing her left hand on his left hand as he decided to hold her hand.

They were finally on I-95 and heading north. They were holding hands as Lilly decided to put on the radio, which was playing local news, and the news was talking about the murders that were happening.

"Oh my God...a child was found dead in the backwoods...that's horrible! Lilly said with a disgusted tone.

"I dunno how anyone could hurt a child...Fuckin' piece of shit!" Jack said with an angered tone.

Jack had to use the restroom as the coffee he dranked in the morning was catching up with him.

They arrived at the Augusta Rest Area, pulled the car into the parking, and Jack got out and went inside to use the bathroom. Soon afterward, another person walked in strangely while briefing looking at Lilly.

Jack went inside to urinate and noticed blood smears on the walls, which looked fresh.

Jack raised his eyebrows as he went into the stall nearest to the wall and stood facing the wall as there was no stall door. Nervousness filled him, but he was able to relieve himself.

A sigh of relief came over him, and then he shook it a few times and zipped up; suddenly, there was a knock on the stall next to him, and he thought, *oh shit, someone is trying to get my attention... WHAT THE FUCK!?* He thought.

Jack stepped out of the stall and walked over to the sink to wash his hands, and the sinks were also smudged with blood. He was a little surprised that the rest area was still open as he looked down into one of the trash cans with crumpled yellow tape. It was the tape that police used to mark a crime scene. Another knock was heard, and Jack quickly turned around as water drips fell from his hands.

"Help me, mister." The voice said from one of the stalls. *It sounded like the man was hurt,* as Jack thought, aware it could be a sick joke.

Jack stood cautionary at the stained sink as he stood still, listening and kneeling to see if he could see the man's feet under one of the stalls. He noticed the man was wearing cowboy boots, tan ones with the leather clean and shiny if the man shone his boots every day, but he sensed something was wrong, and the man from the stall kept asking for help, and Jack was thinking, *Fuck you! I will not help you, you weirdo!* Jack thought and turned the other way, towards the exit.

Jack walked to his car and got in while Lilly looked at him with slight concern as Jack was silent. They left the rest area; as they continued on their trip to Lilly's parent's house, the man in the stall came out, and blood was gushing from his neck. As his shirt was covered in blood, Jack didn't know as if he never went to the stall where the man was. The man was near the wall where Jack remained close to the stalls.

His penis had also been pricked, as the person who did it didn't want him to die quickly. His pants absorbed the blood.

As the man was in the restroom, falling and, at one point, almost exited the building, but fell backward and landed back into the restroom while holding himself. He fell to the floor as the smell of urine perversities on the floor was now all over his blood-covered clothes. He heard footsteps.

"Hello, can anyone out there hear me?! I need help! "He said while pleading.

The footsteps stopped, and he heard a car's doors slamming, and then he heard the car drive off onto the pike.

"Fuck me!" He screamed with tears rolling down his face, and then...*I have to get more paper towels; I can't believe I'm fuckin' bleeding to death! Fuckin' guy came and cut me twice while I was pissin.' I don't want to die!*

He went to the bathroom towel dispenser and got paper towels for the cuts, which didn't help much.

Soon, help arrived, and the man survived...

Chapter Seven

Later that day, it rained as the weather report predicted heavy rain with strong winds.

As CMP was restoring power to some towns with reported power outages. The storm continued its' furious rage as Paula Stone was driving her car down the highway near the Auburn exit, which she usually would get off at, but she lived in Auburn and worked for a firm in South Portland.

She made it home with the storm ravaging. Paula got out of the car and ran into her house on the outskirts of Auburn. She wasn't a big city person; she grew up in Beddington, Maine, a small rural town. Paula moved to the south, went to college, and got an excellent job. Her boyfriend, Todd, has been with her for two years. They met in college and have been together ever since.

When she got inside, she threw her clothes on the floor, got nightclothes out of the bedroom drawer, and was ready to shower as she was drenched.

Her house had one couch and two chairs she had bought at Dunn's Furniture for $400 for all three. They were on sale. After the shower, she prepared dinner and reheated the leftover Pizza Hut pizza from last night.

Paula sat on the couch while awaiting her pizza to be somewhat hot. *Re-cooked oven pizza is awesome! Pizza Hut pizza is the best; I'm starving!* She thought. She and Todd went to Pizza Hut in Windham last night for date night.

The pizza was ready, and she got her plate ready; she took the pizza out of the oven with her Mickey Mouse Mit she got from a co-worker who went to Florida two years ago.

The pizza was hot and steamy, like it was fresh, but not too bad for leftover pizza.

She sat on the couch with her freshly re-heated pizza, a glass of wine, and some T.V. She was finally relaxed and enjoying herself the night before her day started all over tomorrow.

Paula relaxed. Todd would be home at five thirty from work.

Todd was at the Augusta rest area after leaving work in Augusta on 119 Crossing Way. He was a manager at the Target store. He thought he could make it home with a full bladder as well as he felt he had to go number two, but he was sadly mistaken.

He was relieving himself during the storm as it continued its fury.

The restroom was almost immaculate, with the help of cleaning crews, but a few stains were still visible.

With everything that has happened here, the rest area remained open.

Some people stopped but moved on because some knew what had happened. It was becoming a creepy tourist attraction.

I wish I could shit, but my ass is staying no, but my fucking mind is saying yes. I hate this place. Let's get going, asshole, and do your job. Todd was thinking while hoping to hurry and leave the rest area. The door opened, and someone was walking in with rain coming down as he heard squeaky shoes in the restroom.

Todd was in the second stall while he sat nervously with no door on the stall, and Todd kept his private parts covered up. The man used the stall next to him, and the guy pushed his pants down, sat down on the toilet seat, and relieved himself first; then gas was released, and then a significant slash. Todd heard the guy sigh in relief, and Todd almost chuckled but held it in and was eager to get out and be on his way, but suddenly he was going, and he, too, had a sigh of relief. The man beside him heard him and giggled a little, saying, "Welcome to the club, pal!" The man said with a chuckle.

Todd was finished as he was anxious to finish up and get going. Suddenly, the lights went out, and the man in the next stall yelled, "What the fuck!? Who shut the fucking lights off!?"

"Turn them back on, assholes!" He yelled, and Todd remained quiet, wondering if the man was blaming him for the prank; then, "Oh, fuck no. Please don't...No!!!" The man in the next stall screamed as there were ripping sounds and screaming...Todd slowly got his pants on and zipped up.

A moment later, there was whimpering from the next stall, and Todd stood in the stall, keeping quiet, waiting to hear something. He could almost hear the man next to him whimpering and then the watery sounds as if someone was squeezing an orange and then felt wetness by his feet; his first thought was, this guy fucking urinated all over the floor? Or was it blood? Todd had a pack of matches on him (which he occasionally smokes but was trying to quit).

He lit one match using the stall wall, and he knelt, seeing blood all over the floor, and the base of the toilet he was on was capped with blood. The match almost burned his fingers as he stood there thinking about what to do. He was shaking all over, knowing that the man next was dead and *the killer was still around or was it a suicide or just some fuckin' trick!?* Todd nervously thought.

The truth eluded Todd from seeing it, and he tried to listen if he could hear something or someone moving around, but he couldn't. The only sounds he heard were his feet sticking to the blood as the air got to them as if it would stain his sneakers.

Todd tried another match and lit it.

He walked out of the stall while holding the burning match and slowly looked around while he clenched his fists, and he was ready. The match went out, and Todd lit another one. He used his thumb to ignite it and saw blood all over the floor, and then, someone took a breath behind him and blew out the match.

He realized that someone was behind him, and he swung around with his right fist, hoping to make contact, and sure enough, he hit something, and he heard a big thump. He knew he had knocked the person down, and then Todd ran for the door without lighting a match; he ran and slipped on the bloody floor, and suddenly he heard footsteps slowly moving towards him with the person's shoes or sneakers, making that sticky sound and Todd lied on the floor, feeling wet all over and was hurting a little as he felt pain in his right hip. He used his hands and pushed himself up while looking for the matches to see who was in the restroom.

The sounds of the footsteps were unbearable as he knew someone was walking towards him; he tried to get up but kept slipping and feeling the aching hip pain as he kept hearing the footsteps, and then, there were none! He got up slowly while holding his hip, and the location of the matches was nowhere to be found.

Blood smeared all over his back and the rest of his body, mixed with the rain. The wetness was truly disgusting.

He waited for the person, but nothing happened. Suddenly, someone comes in, and the person turns the lights on, and the man sees Todd standing, holding his hip and covered with blood on the floor, trying to get up covered with blood. The man ran out and called the police while Todd stood still, feeling the pain, and he looked at the stall and saw the man's insides had been spilled all over the floor. He did wonder, though. *Who the hell was the other person in here who killed that guy?* Todd thought while slowly crawling out, and he would call Paula and tell her what happened while the man that walked in called the police. ...

Chapter Eight

Todd went home after calling her and talked to Paula about the incident; he told her the whole story, and she asked him about calling the police, but he said that the man that walked in and was on the phone with them. The police interviewed him, and then he went to the hospital, where he was checked out. Hours later, he could go home while smelling like piss and blood.

That night. The rest area was closed for another homicide. A Super Shine cleaning company would come in forty-eight hours later to clean the mess. This, of course, was at the Governor's orders. They cleaned the restrooms as the police permitted, as the CSI had gathered clues, but they never found the person responsible for the murder of the man in the stall.

Chapter Nine

Ted was sick in bed with the flu, vomiting some things he never knew he had in his system, and the rest of the family was gone. He had been sick with the flu for three days.

Ted had gathered the little strength he could summon, and he got up and walked into the living room, where the whole house was quiet except for the gloomy weather, as it was raining.

He had a blanket wrapped around him as he shivered uncontrollably.

Ted sat down in the recliner. His face was pale, and he was fragile. He felt he had lost some weight but had only been sick for a few days. The abundance of vomiting and having the runs are an incredible diet for some people. A red plastic bucket, along with flushable wipes and ginger ale, were his best friends. Without warning, he would rush to the bathroom and simultaneously exclude bodily fluids from both ends, which was remarkably exhausting. He had fallen asleep as his paleness journeyed into the night, where he was met with Terri, who checked his vitals and adjusted his blanket as he would deal with spontaneous chills.

Ted was in and out of sleep. His eyes were heavy, while his body felt frail and fragile. If his sickness had continued, Terri would have taken him to the hospital or called the rescue. The kids were also concerned as they ate dinner and occasionally checked on their sickened father.

He shifted his body in the recliner as, at times, his 'blanky' would hang over the edge and get caught on the metal frame of the recliner. Ted dreamt of walking out into the rain and riding a bike. This was the same bike he rode as a kid. He rode his bike during a rainstorm while waiting for his father to come home from work.

It was three in the morning, and Ted woke up with nausea and, sure enough, another trip to the bathroom.

What the fuck is this? When will the hell this stop? I feel like shit!

This fuckin' flu is draining my life, starting with my bodily fluids and what's next...rash on my ass! He thought with an exhausting tone.

He noticed some blood on his shirt. He immediately checked his mouth as making another trip to the bathroom and quickly checked his mouth and there was nothing except the half-digested mucus in the corners of his mouth.

Three more days passed as he kept the 'blood' finding to himself and never revealed it to Terri as he knew she would force him to go to the hospital. He wiped his mouth and walked into the kitchen while the weakness troubled his body. He forced himself to chew crackers, only to regurgitate them into the toilet.

The next few days, Ted started to feel better, as he had been out of work for five days, and then, he was able to return to work without having that 'vomit' feeling in his throat as he fed on burned toast and dranked warm coke and ginger ale.

Chapter Ten

Ted was back at work. He opened three accounts since coming back to work. Leaves blew by the bank windows as he liked the different colors as they would hit the ground, only later to be blown off or racked by yard workers.

Terri got home from work, threw down her purse and work bag, and turned on the answering machine, listening to see if there were any messages from the State Police, but there were none.

Only one message was from Ted, saying he was going to Walmart to pick up a few things he needed, like shaving cream, Imodium AD, body spray, toothpaste, and some milk. Terri thought, *Oh crap! He's going out to get those things, and I was just at the store three days ago.*

Terri layed on the couch and was grateful that Ted was trying to help with groceries, but she had already gotten them. She smiled while watching TV and felt relaxed after a busy day at work. She had a glass of wine. Red wine was her favorite.

Terri's eyes grew tired as she knew the girls would be home any minute. She decided to close her eyes and take a nap. Her glass of red wine was half empty as it sat on the coffee table, with a couple of drips sliding down from the rim where her lips had touched.

Ted got to Wal-Mart. He went inside the store, grateful that he had brought his long overcoat as the air grew chilly.

"How are you doing today, sir," The cashier asked. Ted glanced at him with the items he wanted and sat on the rolling belt.

"Good; how are you doing?" Ted replied.

"My life sucks, and I'm underpaid. Does that tell you anything?" The cashier said while scanning the items. The cashier had long greasy hair with his tongue pierced; Ted saw it while the clerk was talking. He also had the traditional blue vest saying, *Everything for less at Wal-Mart!* Along with the cashier's name tag, which read, 'Buck.'

He also had many buttons on his vest promoting new releases such as movies and toys.

"Well, I'm sorry that your life sucks," Ted said while reaching for his wallet to pull out his debit card.

"Well, when you're working here and only making $14.25 an hour, you get slightly irritated with everything." The cashier finished scanning the items and gave Ted a disgust like *what the fuck do you do for a living, you cocksucker!* The cashier thought and judged Ted by his handsome suit with combed hair.

"I'm sorry you feel that way, man" Ted stood in front of the card machine, waiting for the cashier to give the total.

"It's $22.50, sir," He said calmly while eyeing Ted's wallet. Ted pulled out the card, slid it through, and the cashier pressed the button to ask for *debit or credit.* Ted pushed the credit button and asked him if the amount was ok, and he pushed yes, and the cashier gave him the receipt.

"Have a good night, sir."

"You too," Ted said, and the cashier didn't even say thank you or thank you for shopping at Wal-Mart. Ted shrugged it off, grinning a little.

Ted got into his car and left while the glowing blue letters of Walmart shined in his rearview mirror.

***

There has been another murder at the Augusta Rest Area. As of right now, the police have no suspects. The reporter said while interviews were being conducted, especially with Det. Mitchell.

The reporter asked Det. Mitchell about a potential serial killer.

"Detective, do you think there's a serial killer?" She asked while there were microphones from all directions as Det. Mitchell stood outside the rest area as the police decided to shut it down for the time being.

"I don't want to use that term, but if all of these cases are related, we have someone who can't stop."

"Why is the serial killer using this particular rest area?" Another report asked Det. Mitchell felt out of place as he would rather be doing his work than being asked questions.

"As of right now, we don't know. Not all of the murders are happening here, but we still don't know. That's all I have to say for now," he thanked the reporters and left.

***

That night, Ted didn't go home. He was starting to get another headache. He decided to get a drink. He went straight to Jim's Bar in Portland, had a few beers, and watched some sports on the TV.

The bar was located right in the Old Port, not too far from Holiday Inn, just about one mile. It was a decent place to drink, and he never called or texted Terri to tell her where he was going. He figured she would figure it out as he's done this before. *Terri should be ok with this, as I've done it before. Hell, she's done it with me when going out with her co-workers, so fuck it!* He thought while sitting at the bar and drinking a beer.

Jim Knowles was 47. He'd been in the bar business for twenty years, and always enjoyed the atmosphere. He had a good football physique but never played football in school. He wrestled for Portland High School and was the only African American on the team. He won some matches but blew his knee out in his senior year, and it ruined his chances of earning a scholarship.

"Jim, I need another beer," Ted said while watching the tube.

"You've already had four, and you still have to drive home, pal," Jim said while wiping the bar table with a clean rag.

"Come on, man. I need another drink; my son is still missing." Ted glanced at Jim with a slight tear in his right eye, indicating that drinking was his way of dealing with the mystery of not knowing where his son was.

Jim looked at him and gave him one more beer, but that was it!

"One more before hitting the road, Ted. You need to go home!" Jim said with a firm tone as he could see Ted was distressed due to his son's disappearance.

Jim gave Ted the beer and told him, "That's your last one, pal. No more after that!" Jim said firmly, and Ted nodded while taking a drink.

Ted knew he had some groceries out in the car, and almost the milk wouldn't spoil due to the cold air outside that would keep everything cool. Ted sat at the stool, realizing it was late, and Terri would be pissed about him coming home late.

He left the bar half an hour after having his last drink while Jim slowly escorted him out. He took Ted outside, making sure he could stand, which Ted was, but his speech was a little slurry, and thanked Jim for the beers. Jim nodded and went back inside the bar.

Ted slowly walked to his car while feeling very drunk and unsure if he could drive home or sit in the car and fall asleep. *Maybe...I should..ld...sta..y and...wai...t to get...betta...Ted* thought he was a little drunk, but he could start his car and warm it up.

The car took five minutes to warm up. He took a bottle of Coke out of the bag of groceries that were not on the list he wanted to buy, but he was glad he did. He twisted the cap off and started drinking from it. He wanted to go home but wasn't sure if he could get there.

He slowly drove (wandered) on his way home and was finally, after only driving 40 miles an hour, with no cops in sight. He was home at 2:30

in the morning. He parked his car at a crooked angle and slumped over the driver's side, almost thankful that he made it and never got pulled over.

He grabbed his things and groceries and went inside the house where no one was up, and he crashed on the couch with the milk in the fridge and the rest on the counter as he drifted off into sleep.

The following day, Terri was at his feet, and she looked concerned as she watched him sleep and wondered how drunk he was from last night. *The damn fool probably came home after smelling like a bar and crashed on the couch.* She smiled a little as she looked down at him with his mouth open, like a dog sleeping with saliva running down his mouth.

Terri started making breakfast as the kids were up, and she knew Ted would wake up with a hangover.

That morning. They got a call from the police, the investigation was off, and Sean was gone; they had no more time and no evidence. The police officer spoke with a remorseful tone. After informing Terri, the cordless phone was still left in her hand as she slid down the wall and sat on the cold kitchen floor, and she just stared at the wall. Her breakfast was not being cooked as it sat on the kitchen counter while the police officer could hear asking Terri if she was alright. She lifted the phone to her lips and sadly whimpered, "Yes, I'm ok." The phone conversation ended, and her hand dropped to the floor while the phone sat in the palm of her hand, almost rolling onto the floor.

Tears rolled out. She sat on the cold kitchen floor, shaking in shock, and wondered what had happened to the investigation. She didn't know how to tell Ted because he would be furious over this, considering the investigators had told them they would find Shawn regularly and everything would be back to normal, *but how do you define normal?* She tearfully thought.

Terri knew she had to gather her thoughts and wake Ted from his drunken sleep.

She sat on the floor, and the phone was now on her lap with the ringing going off, indicating; that the phone had been taken off the hook. She pictured Sean lying in a ditch, reaching for help as if she was standing on the side of the road, but she couldn't help him; it was as if he was in another world, but she could see him but not touch him.

Her hopeful face turned pale and cumbersome bags developed beneath her eyes.

Her body remained motionless as she was paralyzed with shock and sadness.

An inevitable spike of hatred started to build within her, and those tears were no longer filled with sadness and lost hope but with anger and not giving up. She slowly got up, revealing her underwear to the world by sliding up the wall, and the phone rolled down to the right. She put the phone on the hook, and she went into the living room slowly as if she was in the movie *Night Of The Living Dead, The original 1968 version made by George Romero.*

She saw Ted sleeping comfortably and stood over him as if scanning him with her angered but sad eyes.

Ted woke up, and his eyes were burning with the alcohol he had consumed last night; it was more like he had devoured. He saw Terri standing over him, and, at first, he thought *she was mad at him about last night,* but he suddenly read her face like it was a map of emotions filled with despair, sadness, and anger.

"Oh, my God! He's dead! Isn't he?" Ted got up shouting.

"They can't find him. They called this morning and said they're giving up the investigation." She murmured while trying to fight new tears rolling down her already pale cheeks.

"What do you mean? What did they say?" He asked while standing in front of her, waiting for the answer he didn't want to hear, but he knew.

"They're giving up the investigation, and they feel there's nothing they can do now because of lack of evidence." She cooed while looking down at the floor, and her tears were trickling down, and some were hitting the floor.

"No!" Ted fell to his knees as he cried and screamed. He trembled as he let it all out.

"Those FUCKS! THEY GAVE US HOPE IN FINDING HIM!" Ted cried and screamed.

He swore and banged his fist against the wall and made a dent.

Terri stood motionless and looked at Ted with more tears trickling down her pale cheeks, and her emotions were gone. The shock was gone. She knelt to gain her strength and held him; at first, he didn't want to hold her, but she grabbed him, and then he grabbed her, and they held each other tightly for most of the morning.

Chapter Eleven

Lyle Johnson lived in New Gloucester most of his life, working as a gas station attendant at Wings on Lewiston Road near Mario's and the post office.

He was 51 and made $11.25 an hour. Pumping gas was something he enjoyed very much; he never knew why he felt that way, but it was his feeling to help out. He knew a lot of people that stopped there. He knew the faces and the names and people regarding their personalities.

The owner of Wings always enjoyed watching Lyle, who enjoyed being around people. The owner was planning on making Lyle a manager, but so far, he has been unsuccessful in finding someone to replace him.

Having dirty blonde hair, forest green eyes, and a heavy build as if he had worked in the lumber all his life, but he never had; his build was natural. His naturally ripped jeans, a style he liked, always bought a pair every other month, especially after payday.

"Lyle, you're shift is almost up." The owner said while helping a customer with their dense gas can outside near their vehicle.

"All right. Let me finish helping this woman, and then I'll go."

Lyle finished pumping the gas, gave him the cash, fifteen dollars, and exact change, and left. Lyle went into the store, carded out, said goodbye to the owner, got into his pickup truck, and went home.

Driving around in an '85 red pickup truck was his joy. He lived by himself, but he never stayed home much except to sleep and shower, but most of the time, he was always eating out either at Denny's in Auburn or at Cole Farms in Gray.

As the weather was a little chilly, he drove off and went home on Bald Hill Road past the recycling plant.

He lived in a trailer and had about two acres of land.

He got home and got out of his truck. He opened the door to his home and always kept his place clean as he hoped he would get company, which was a rarity. Lyle was a friendly person, but some that he was a loner, based on how he carried himself. He was quiet for the most part and didn't interact with the surrounding neighbors.

That night, he dozed off in his recliner, which was brand new. He bought it from Marden's in Gray three months ago. The recliner was $100, the original price was $500, and it was discontinued and never used. He bought the recliner with saved-up bottle money, and his boss also gave him a small bonus.

He dreamt he had met a young woman in her late twenties, and she had long, dirty blonde hair like him, watching the sunset at Old Orchard Beach. *You are so beautiful...*he said with a dreamy tone.

It was one in the morning. Suddenly, Lyle woke up due to remembering one thing he had to do at night: get everything ready for the next day.

The person who worked that day usually would have to take care of it, but when Lyle was down the road, the owner liked him a lot considering him to be a likable and reliable worker.

He got up, just wearing his jeans. He just threw on and left as he got into his truck, and he was a little cold as autumn air chilled him. He arrived at the store and saw a person near the street just in front of the shop, and there was no other vehicle around, but Lyle thought, *some teenager hanging around smoking dope or just plain drunk.*

He pulled his truck in front of the store and noticed the pumps had been shut off; *Bob must have already done it.* Lyle got out of his truck and got his keys out that dangled with other keys from his belt at the waist. Lyle felt that his responsibility to protect the store while the owner was not around. Lyle had nothing else to care for in life.

He got to the store's front door, and he knew someone was standing in the light, but he couldn't see the face to make out the person. Lyle felt as if the person was up to something, good or bad. The uneasiness filled him.

He slid the key into the lock, and it wouldn't turn. He tried again, but nothing. He knew he had the correct key because it was the same one he'd used for many years, and the locks had never been changed.

He heard footsteps behind him; he quickly turned and realized the person standing at the street light was gone. He turned around again to the lock and had no luck, but the footsteps started up again, and then he looked at him again, but nothing. *What the hell is going on? This key should work...*Lyle thought and stopped what he was doing, and he decided to go home and call the owner.

He walked back to his truck and realized the footsteps were near. He grabbed a wrench from the trunk of his truck, flashed the flashlight around, and saw nothing.

He walked around the store with a flashlight in his hand while seeing no one around. An 18-wheeler s drove by, heading north, and scared Lyle briefly. He decided to leave and call the owner when he got home.

He headed back to the truck. As he got in and realized the missing cigarette lighter, someone suddenly grabbed him by the throat from the backseat on the driver's side, and the person smeared the lighter into his neck. Lyle screamed with terror; as he tried to fight the person, he hit a person with the wrench, knocking the person down on the ground as the attacker got out of the truck. Lyle rushed to get his keys, but they fell out of his hands, and he had no idea where they were. The pain from the cigarette lighter was piercing, but he could handle it.

He knelt by his feet with his left hand and found the keys. The attacker got up and ran into the truck, and Lyle felt a sharp, piercing object going into his neck. Lyle screamed, gripping his throat as he looked outside and saw the attacker staring at him while his face remained in the darkness. Lyle felt blood rushing, thrusting from his neck as Lyle started to get out; he tried to stand but fell to the ground. He started to crawl, trying to grab the attacker's shoes, but Lyle realized that the attacker was wearing cowboy boots.

Lyle kept fighting while feeling red ooze covering his body, and Lyle was dying.

Lyle tried to crawl more, but weakness overtook him, and Lyle tried to reach the boots of the attacker, and then, Lyle reached out one last time while fresh gushing blood stained the tard payment and then...

"You got blood on my boots, boy! Death has your reservation, and your number is up! Oh, by the way, tell 'em, Duke sent you!" Lyle died minutes later, and that morning the owner found him, and there was blood all over the side of the truck on the driver's side, and the tarred pavement had a pool of blood beside the truck. Lyle was found with his face down, and the owner cried as he knelt a couple of feet away from Lyle's body, and then he got up and called the police. Wings were closed for the rest of the day.

Chapter Twelve

The Augusta Rest Area was open. A month passed, and the murders were sporadic while the State Police didn't know where to start; technically, because the killer or killers were ingenious in leaving no clues for the police as if they knew the process and how long it would take to solve the case or find suspects.

The police were clueless about the case, as the murders were no longer concentrated in one location.

Det. Paul Mitchell sat in his home office, where he enjoyed doing much of his work.

Being at the barrack's office stressed him out too much, and he had to be somewhere where he could think, and *home was where the heart was.* He thought while his 12-year-old daughter, Elisa, was on her cell doing Tik Tok. His wife, Jennifer, died five years ago of Crohn's Disease. The disease perforated a hole in the upper region of her colon, and she died within six hours. Jennifer suffered, but only death brought relief. Paul's eyes watered as he thought about that night. *Easter morning, and one moment, we were playing games late at night with the three of us, and the next, she was in pain.* Tears streamed down his cheeks as he also remembered that Jennifer refused to go to the hospital for many hours until Paul forced her, and the three of them spent Easter in the hospital.

The disease flared up, and she was rushed to the hospital with vomiting and stomach pains.

Only to discover Crohn's had perforated and made a quarter-sized hole in her colon near the small intestine. She had the disease for ten years and was on numerous medications with endless hospital visits on her 'medical' resume.

Paul thought about her every day and how she was much happier at home than in the hospital and getting little rest. Elisa handled the loss by journalling and barely speaking to her father.

"Holy shit! This case is something." Paul said out loud while talking to himself; it helped him think.

A kid is missing, and eight murders, somehow all around this rest area, but now, that's changed! The homicide at that gas station in New Gloucester took me for a loop. I think we need to get a specialist who can identify serial killers and maybe develop a profile. Det. Mitchell thought, getting the feeling the homicide in New Gloucester was connected.

"Dad, I'm going to bed." Paul jumped out of his office chair, startled by his daughter's sudden appearance.

"Crap, Elisa, you scared the crap out of me!"

"Sorry, Dad. I thought you heard me standing here in the doorway?" She said with a slight smile as if it was humorous, scaring her father.

"No! You know me, wrapped in my work."

"I know, Dad. At least you're home," She murmured while walking over to him and kissing him on the forehead, and Paul kissed her back. And then she walked back into the hallway and went to bed.

He sat back down, glancing at his file with the red dots on the map he printed out, and he saw that most of the murders were at the rest area and only two were not. *What's the connection? I wonder if there are one or two killers... Maybe.* Det. Mitchell thought.

"Oh, boy, this case had no witnesses and no suspects. No trace of the suspect's prints or blood, not even a footprint...Who is this guy?" Paul stared at the map and compared it to the file, and this was growing by the day. The phone rings, and Paul got up and goes to it.

"Hello." He answered sternly, knowing it was the department calling him.

"Oh shit, another murder! Oh, right, I'll be right there." Paul hangs up the phone and heads for the closet where his leather jacket is hanging. He went upstairs to wake up Elisa, and she was not even sleeping. He told her he had to go and would be back; she nodded.

Det. Mitchell lived in Gray, and it would take forty-five minutes to get to Augusta. While driving, he took the Lewiston Road north, got on the Auburn Exit, and merged onto the turnpike. While driving, he thought about who the victim might be as it was Capt. Morse had called and told him, but she never mentioned age, sex, or who found the victim. *All this was important as I needed to figure out a profile.* As he got closer to Augusta, EZ-Pass paid the toll, and he was close as he made turns and then had to get on I-95.

Paul saw the coroner was already there, and he saw that Capt. Morse was there also with state troopers. He got out of his car and walked over to her. The body was not moved as ordered by Capt. Morse as she waited for Paul to show up.

"Holy shit! So much blood!" A Maine State trooper said while trying to hold his insides in after walking out of the restroom and over to Det Mitchell and Capt Morse.

"This is what a crime scene looks like...bloody!" Paul said while looking at the trooper and thinking...*Rookie.*

Blood was splattered all over the tile walls, and the floor was smeared with footsteps, thanks to the state troopers and local law enforcement. Paul walked through the scene trying to find clues and saw something near the first stall that looked like a nail clipper. He pulled out his latex gloves and put them on, then knelt, gently picked it up with blood dripping off it, and placed it in a plastic baggie.

He walked outside the rest area and told one of the state troopers he wanted the area closed until further notice. The trooper nodded while looking at Capt. Morse and she nodded.

Paul hung around the scene, continuing to look for anything as the body was inside the men's restroom, but Paul decided to wait and not touch the body based on possible evidence being disturbed.

A Channel 10 news van pulled into the rest area, and a reporter and her film crew rushed towards Paul and Capt. Morse.

Jen Fairfield was a prominent reporter on Channel 10 news. She covered news such as the Oak Hills Apartments fire two years ago, and the result was; the owner burned down his building to get insurance money while making forty families homeless.

"Detective? Detective...Can you answer us?" She was running over to him with her TV crew, and he thought, *great! Now we're having fun!* Paul thought while looking at Capt Morse.

"Yes," he said while looking down at the ground and trying to sketch a statement in his head; he was afraid he would mess it up!

Jen she started to get the microphone, barely looking at Paul or making small talk while the crew was getting ready with the camera.

"Hurry up. You idiots, we don't have all night!" She shouted, and everyone in their thoughts was saying...*Bitch!*

"Are we ready yet?" She said sarcastically. One of the camera guys said, "almost."

"Hurry up, or we'll lose the time," She said while looking at them and holding her microphone in front of her while Paul was thinking as he stood there waiting for the news crew to set up and have this reporter standing next to him. *Will someone please shoot me? Or shoot this bitch next to me.* Paul thought as he hated reporters and Capt. Morse let him handle this.

"Are we on yet?" She asked impatiently while the camera crew was almost ready.

"We're on." One of them said.

"About damn time, you idiot!" She said while fixing her hair.

"All right. Five, four, three, two." The camera rolls, and "Hi, this is Jen Fairfield with Channel 10 news. We're on the scene of another brutal murder at the Augusta Rest Area, and standing next to me is Det. Paul Mitchell. Detective, can you tell us what happened here? And do you have any clues on the motive or suspects?"

She asked while awaiting a response from him. He stood there, barely blinking and looking at her while she was two inches shorter than him.

"The clues that we have right now suspect that we may have a serial killer out there, and his primary focus has been rest areas, especially this one, and that people should know that when going into a rest area for sleep, going to the bathroom or *fuck another guy;* take extreme caution when entering the area. As of right now, this rest area is closed due to further investigation; thank you." He walked off camera and headed back to the scene. Jen tried to interview Capt. Morse.

"Capt. Morse, what are your thoughts?" Jen asked while Capt. Morse looked at her and said, "As of right now, we have no suspects, nor do we think these murders are different. We're dealing with someone who likes rest areas, particularly this one. That's all for now. Thank you." Capt. Morse walked away and joined Det. Mitchell.

Paul returned to the scene but quickly walked to his car and took a break. He stood by his car, almost leaning on it, watching the scene being dissected and disrupted as more TV crews showed up and Capt. Morse walked over to him. She leaned up against his car next to him and said, "Well, that went well." She smiled.

"I'm sorry for swearing on the air."

"No worries unless I'll hear from the Governor herself, but I think we might be alright." She said with a certain reassurance.

"Heading home?" Capt. Morse asked while placing her hair in a ponytail; the smell of her perfume was soothing to Paul. He looked at her and wanted to ask her to get a drink, but he knew that would not be appropriate.

"Yeah, I'm heading home. Elisa is home alone, and I need to get back." He said while sitting up, walking to the driver's side, and getting into his car.

"Alright, I'll see you tomorrow."

Paul nodded and drove off while reporters took pics of him leaving while news media interviewed Capt. Morse.

Chapter Thirteen

The kitchen table seemed empty without Shawn being around, and Ted was reminded of it every day and thought of how he could have fallen asleep for almost an hour, and his son was gone just like that.

Ted had thought of putting a gun to his head because of the guilt and that he should have been a much better father than he was on that dreadful day. *I can't believe I had fallen asleep, and within that time, Shawn was taken...*

He sat at the kitchen table looking at his two girls and was grateful he didn't screw that up with the girls and lost them. Terri glanced at him, seeing him disturbed and feeling guilty while she was sad and somewhat blamed Ted for falling asleep, but she loved him and couldn't place all the blame on him. *Things would have been different if I had been in the car rather than hanging around in the back.* She thought while taking a drink of her iced water.

The kitchen became silent as everyone was sad that morning. The whereabouts of Shawn echoed harshly as all hope of finding him was gone. Ted glanced at the dish with bacon, eggs, and toast, and he rested his hand gently on his coffee cup that said, 'I Love Banking!' It had a smiley face on it, and Ted got sick to his stomach like he was going in for a colonoscopy and had to drink Fleet-Phosphate, *yummy...*He thought to himself.

"How about all of us go for a drive today?" Ted suggested trying to rid himself of some guilt as it was eating him alive. The family agreed, and they went to New Hampshire and went to visit the scenery up there.

"This would be good for us as they have the mountains are always pretty, and there are many places to visit, such as Santa's Village, Canobie Lake, and Old Man on the mountain (or what's left before it fell apart)," Terri said while smiling a little as the family agreed.

That morning they got ready and headed out as they knew this day the trip would be suitable for them all and much needed.

Shawn's absence in the car could be felt as the girls were on their phones, and Terri was on hers, quiet and reserved. Ted was quiet but hopeful that this day trip would help ease some of the temporary sadness.

Ted was driving while looking at his wife steadily, knowing her agony.

I know she blames me for Shawn's disappearance. It is my fault that he was taken. I take the blame for that, but some BASTARD took him! How is that my fault!? Ted thought while driving, and they were entering New Hampshire. They decided to head to North Conway. The scenic route was a pleasurable experience. They stopped at stores, did some shopping, and ate at the Applebees near Lowe's.

***

Two weeks passed, and there had been no murders. The State decided to reopen the rest area. Some visitors were hesitant about going into it based on the recent murders that have darkened that site. For others, some were stopping by and taking pictures and posting them on social media.

Fred Deer and Hank Robbins were two custodians who cleaned the rest area daily. They traveled together and worked for the State. One week, they would take Fred's truck, and the following week, they would take Hank's car.

Fred Deer grew up in Durham, Maine. He had lived on a farm with his mother and stepfather and had a little brother who died of colon cancer at eleven.

Fred was an old-fashion farmer who didn't believe in using technology like computers and high-tech farm equipment for hay and raising farm animals as other farmers do.

Hank was the opposite. He loved technology and loved computers. He also ran his computer business out of his residence in Durham, Maine. Hank and Fred lived three miles apart from each other.

It was a cloudy day with rain in the forecast, as Fred was hurrying to get his work done for the day and then could rest for the night until to-morrow. *Rains' coming. Better hurry it up and finish; I don't want to get stuck in a downpour.* Fred thought that while cleaning the men's restroom, Hank was cleaning the women's restroom.

Fred finished in time before it rained, and then it was pouring. Hank was a little behind as a few visitors came in, and Hank walked out of re-spect for the female presence.

Hank walked over to Fred, who was in the back under the metal-roof tent, and they both watched the rain pour.

"Are you almost done?" Fred asked while smoking a cig, and he gave Hank one.

"I was halfway done, but so many damn people are coming in!" Hank said with a frustrated tone.

"That happens when the fuckin' State reopened this place...it became a spectacle."

"All I know, I want to go home, put some birds on the grill and have a damn beer," Hank said while taking a puff.

"I'll be over then, pal!" Fred smiled, and they both chuckled.

"Well, we can't do this forever. Fuck it... do what you can, and let's get out of here!" Frank suggested, and Hank nodded.

Hank walked back to the women's restroom and did what he could do, and they left.

They had Fred's truck and headed home as Fred would be dropping off Hank at his house.

"You comin' over?" Hank asked, unsure if Fred was coming over or if he was kidding.

"Shit, man! I'll come over! Let me go home and shower, and then I'll be over," Fred said, and Hank said, "Okay."

Fred dropped off Hank and headed home. He arrived and parked his truck, and got out. He walked over to the farm and looked at his animals. With his roughed eyes, his white beard glanced at the farmland and had hoped not to work but farm, but the farm was high, and he needed to work outside to provide for himself.

Frank thought about his life while leaning on the cow patch fence and watching his cows eat grass. He had horses, chickens, and two roosters. He wore his hat, saying, 'I'm old but hanging.'

He walked to his house and decided to get into the shower and head to Hank's place afterward. Hank was his best friend. *Shit, workin' together for eight years and hangin' out outside, the guy was almost like a brother. He was there for me when I went through my divorce. The wifey left me because I could not have kids, so she found a guy who could.* Fred thought while finishing and started to get ready.

He got dressed while sitting on his bed, brushing his hair, which was partially long, while some bald spots were showing. He got up, walked downstairs to the kitchen, grabbed a beer, and sat on the couch while waiting for a little before heading out.

I'm sure hank needs time before I come over and eat all his food. Fred smiled, picked up the TV remote, and turned the TV on. The can of Budweiser was gripped gently in his calloused hand as he watched TV. He had an antenna on his roof and had local TV playing.

He took a sip, and the local news was on. He turned the volume up, and they were talking about 'The Rest Area Killer.' Fred frowned at the name of the killer they gave, as it was a little 'simple.' *Damn! You would think with all those highly educated people, they would come up with a better name.* Fred thought while taking a drink and continued to watch TV.

Fred did have a cell phone. Hank bought it for him as a Birthday gift three years ago. Fred liked it as it was a prepaid phone through Straight

Talk. Fred only paid $30 annually for it. He gave Hank the money for it as Hank paid his bills online.

"Well, gotta go!" Fred shouted as he got up, walked into the kitchen, and grabbed more beer for the road. *Since he's feedin' suppa,' I will bring the refreshments.* Frank thought while smiling and getting into his truck while glaring at his horses.

He drove over while the remaining beer sat nicely on the passenger side with the beer secured by the plastic tie. Before leaving, he saw a black Ford Ranger pulling out of Hank's driveway.

Who the fuck was that!? Fred thought while pulling into the driveway and watching the Ford Ranger drive down the road. Fred knew Hank had some relatives, but *they lived in Vermont. That truck had Maine license plates.* Frank thought while grabbing the beer and going to Hank's front door.

He knocked on the front door while the plastic-tied beer swung loosely in his left hand, and he awaited for Hank to open the door and welcome him in. After waiting a few minutes, Fred figured he might be in the shower. *Maybe the old timer is in the shower or something...I hate to see him answer the door with his nakedness...that would be an awful sight.* Fred thought and reached down to check if the door was unlocked; to his surprise, it was.

"Hank? It's Fred? Are you here?" Fred walked in while holding a six-pack of beer onto the hardwood floor in the living room and then into the kitchen, where he saw that the fridge was partially open.

Fred placed the beer onto the marvel counter, walked over to the half-open fridge, and opened it. He saw that the chicken was in the fridge and Hank had some beers, but then he heard something upstairs.

Fred closed the fridge door abruptly and ran upstairs. He had only been in Hank's house a few times, let alone upstairs, one other time, and a concerned look grew on his bearded face.

"Hank!? Hank? It's Fred…where are you?" Fred searched the bedroom. The covers on the bed were slightly disturbed, and he heard a **THUMP** in the bathroom.

Fred rushed to the bathroom, and the shower was on with the door slightly open, "Hank, it's Fred. Are you ok?" Fred asked while gently pushing the bathroom, and Fred saw Hank lying in the bathroom tub with hot water pelting his bloody face.

"HOLY SHIT!" Fred shouted and ran to his fallen friend. Fred shut the water, almost burning his hand, and he looked at Hank, who was bleeding, and Fred looked down and saw blood running out of his testicles; Hank was still alive and trying to move his lips.

"Hank, don't say anything! "I'll call the police!" Hank grabbed Fred's right arm and held him as Fred watched in horror, and then…Hank was gone. Fred screamed with tears, and he got up and ran to the bathroom, where he saw Hank's cell on the bed and called 9-11.

Durham doesn't have a police department, so either county or state police respond to an emergency call. This time, the Cumberland County Sheriff's Department showed up and rescue.

The rescue came in while Fred sat on the bed with watery eyes, and the rescue was pronounced dead.

A Sheriff asked Fred what had happened, and Fred explained what he saw and their plans for the evening.

A Sheriff and Fred walked down the stairs with Fred in tears, and two other Sheriffs showed up, and they came up on Fred and escorted him to the front of the house.

"Did you see anyone else in the house?" The same Sheriff had been asking Fred questions as he wanted to cover all the basics.

"The only thing I saw while arriving was a black Ford Ranger, but that was it."

"Did you see the license plate, and what state was it in?" The Sheriff asked while writing down the info on a pad.

"The truck had Maine license plates, but I couldn't see the numbers or letters...it was like all scribbled out," Fred said while leaning up against one of the cruisers, and then, he asked to stick as detectives were on their way. Fred stood by, looking at the ground while tears to the frosted ground.

Chapter Fourteen

Det. Mitchell arrived at Hank's house with Fred leaning up against his truck, trembling as the rescue ensured he would be ok. Det. Mitchell arrived and was met by Capt. Morse.

A look of distaste was on her face. "I take it that's not a good sign," Det. Mitchell said to her while walking up to the house as she watched him get out of his car and walk towards her.

"This is not good, Detective. That man over there found his friend dead, but..." her frown face lifted a little, but not much.

"But...what?" Det. Mitchell asked with a confused look.

"That man claims that he saw a black Ford Ranger pulling out of this driveway upon arriving, and it had Maine license plates."

"What's the bad news?"

"The bad news, Detective...the license was scribbled out," the frown face returned after she said that.

Det. Mitchell nodded and looked to the ground in disbelief because this might have been the same killer, but there was no evidence to support that.

"What's the gentleman's name?"

"His name is Fred Deer. As I said, he's the one who saw the truck leaving and found his friend," Capt. Morse explained before Det. Mitchell would head over and interview Fred.

"I gotta say, Captain...this is messed up!" Det. Mitchell said, but Capt. Morse intervened and said, "But, Detective...they *both* work at the Augusta Rest Area part-time, or should I say Mr. Hank Robbins did."

Det. Mitchell nodded and headed over to where Fred was while Capt. The media approached Morse. *Well, that didn't take long,* Capt. Morse thought while deciding to handle the media after Det. Mitchell's 'expressive' interview at the Augusta Rest Area.

"Hello, Mr. Deer?" Det. Mitchell approached Fred, who was shaken up.

"Yes...sir...I am," Fred said while trembling. His eyes were wide, and Paul knew he was shocked.

"I'm Det. Mitchell and I are the lead investigator, and I was wondering if you could tell me what you saw?"

"I already told my story to that Sheriff over there and your Captain as well..." Fred was slightly irritated.

"I understand that, sir, but we have to do this. That way, we have everything we need to investigate and move forward. Again, I'm sorry about this, and I am deeply for your loss. Were you and Mr. Robbins close?" Det. Mitchell asked while jotting down Fred's statement. He interviewed him to ensure his statement remained the same and everything was done accurately.

Fifteen minutes passed, and Det. Mitchell had his statement. Tears flowed down Fred's cheeks as upset.

"Is this related to those murders I've been seeing on the news?" Fred asked while wiping away his tears.

"I can't disclose anything about an ongoing investigation, Mr. Deer. Again, I am sorry about your loss. Please check with the medical staff if you need assistance. Otherwise, you're free to go home," Det. Mitchell said with a remorseful tone.

"I hope you get this fucker! HE KILLED MY FRIEND!"

Det. Mitchell looked at him and nodded. Fred went home while Det. Mitchell walked up to the house and headed in as if he would be welcomed to another homicide.

Chapter Fifteen

The Augusta Rest Area had become a spectacle as tourists from other states, such as Rhode Island, New Hampshire, Massachusetts, and Maryland, wanted to see the rest area for themselves.

Kids ran to the back of the rest area and hung out at one of the benches that used to be shrouded with uncut grass; it was cut clean and repainted now. The Governor saw the tourists' potential and wanted the rest area to look good.

The cold late-October air didn't stop anyone from hanging outside and taking pictures of the 'infamous' murder site. State Trooper Miles Copeland was responsible for securing and keeping the rest area safe.

He sat in his squad car with his 'Cheers' thermos and dranked his coffee. He had a lunch box that was made of metal and had red and white striping. He would make two peanut butter sandwiches with an apple and a homemade brownie (actually, it was made from a box.)

He also had two bottles of water while he sat in his squad car and watched the patrons get out of their cars with smiles of excitement. *This is sad...people coming to a location where innocent people have been murdered, and people are taking joy in that...*He thought with a disgusted look.

Miles worked ten-hour shifts. He was covering this location for six hours at a time, and then, a replacement would show, and Miles would do ticket duty, sitting and scanning cars for speed.

Miles took another sip of his coffee. He had a girlfriend named Georgia. They lived in Fairfield, Maine. Georgia was a Special Ed teacher at the Fairfield Middle School.

There were now ten cars at the rest area, which was becoming almost cluttered. Miles knew he would have to get out and start directing cars and have them either keep going or wait for other drivers to leave. The rest area was not like the rest area in Kennebunk, and it was much smaller.

Miles got out and stood by his cruiser while his eyes gazed at a car filled with college kids, holding their cell phones and eager to take pics. Another car pulled up, and a family of four got out, with three girls and one guy. They were using the facilities.

Miles knew this could be a complicated problem, so he decided to walk to the front of the area while glancing at cars, and then...a black Ford Ranger drove in with Maine license plates. Miles remembered the email he got from Det. Mitchell, regarding a Ford Ranger, was seen at a Durham residence. Miles watched the truck pull in, but the truck driver pulled up to the farthest end and Miles found it suspicious as he decided to walk a little while gazing at the truck.

Miles walked accordingly as he glanced at the truck while vehicles were coming and going. While the driver remained inside, he walked on the sidewalk, trying to be cordial as he stared at the truck. To him, this was odd but not unusual. *Before this spectacle, this was a hot spot for drug dealers, muggings, and guys trying to have a pow-wow with each other. It's impressive how things have drastically changed.* Miles thought he was about to report the truck, but he had to verify the license plates first.

Miles's nerves started to flare up as he approached the truck. As it stood running and the driver was still inside. The odd thing to Miles was that the Ford Ranger windows were tinted as he could not see the driver.

Miles was now standing in front of the truck, and then he looked down at the license plates, which were Maine license plates. Miles tried to look at the numbers/lettering, and the plate was indeed smudged over, as stated by Fred Deer.

Miles knew this was the truck that was reported. Miles reached for his speaker and started to report the truck, but suddenly, the truck's engine shut off. Miles immediately stood guard, walked over to the driver's side, and Miles withdrew his firearm.

"Sir, please get out of the vehicle." There was no response.

"Sir, please get out of the vehicle." There was no response as Miles called for support, and then, the driver's side door slowly opened. Miles gripped his firearm tightly as he quickly looked behind him to see where the visitors had left. There were two other vehicles, one a car and the other a car.

"Sir, please get out of the vehicle," Miles said firmly.

Miles started to walk around the vehicle and glanced at the truck, but suddenly, the door closed, and the truck started up but didn't move. Miles said, "sir, please shut off the vehicle!" Miles said firmly.

"I need backup. I have the vehicle in question at the rest area. I need backup now!" Miles said firmly, and the dispatcher told him backup was on its way.

The truck started to go in reverse, and Miles ordered the truck to stop, and the truck backed up, and Miles yelled at the vehicle to stop.

The truck slowly drove onto the grass and around the back of the rest area. Miles rushed to the truck as he didn't want to fire his firearm until he had a reason. The truck drove around the back, and Miles rushed back, but suddenly, he heard the door slam.

Miles's heart was racing as he kept to his training. He peaked around the corner of the building, and he glanced around and wasn't sure if the driver was still in the truck or not. *HOLY CRAP! I JUST HOPE THE DRIVER IS STILL IN THE TRUCK!?*

Miles held his firearm close to his body as he was peaking around the corner and could see the truck, but he didn't know if the driver was out of the truck or not, but Miles did hear the door slam. *BANG!* Miles was dropped to the ground as he was knocked down by an attacker. Miles tried to fire, but his eyes were hurting, and he tried to call for more backup, but the attacker reached down and cut the wire.

Miles tried to fight, but he was hit with something and yelled, "I NEED HELP!"

"Help is not coming for you, son!" The attacker said as Miles was stabbed in the throat. Miles tried to fight, but he gripped his throat as the pain was piercing, and Miles could not talk.

The attacker slowly walked. Miles was able to glance over and could almost see the attacker walking. The blood gushed out of his throat, and then, he was out.

An hour later, Miles was in the ambulance and was alive. His throat was covered in bandages, and an IV hooked him up. Miles was exhausted and tried to talk, but the paramedics told him not to talk. He was on his way to Maine General Hospital in Augusta.

A couple at the rest area was there with Miles as he lay on the cold ground, bleeding, while other visitors had left. The attacker waited for most of the visitors to leave.

Chapter Sixteen

Stella was a high school senior thinking about going to the dance. *If I can find something to wear, then maybe I'll go.* She thought while standing in front of the mirror and trying different clothes. It was a dance in November that was somewhat big. It wasn't the spring dance, but the dance was called the fall dance.

As Stella Meadows stood in front of the tall mirror in her room while her cell was on the dresser, he was waiting for him to call or text her. Her room was filled with pictures of Justin Bieber, dandelions, and other stuff.

Stella was a straight-A student at Waterville High School and was not popular. She was considered to be an outsider, but she didn't care. She just wanted to go to the dance with a long-time friend, and somewhat she deeply cared for; beyond a friend, and that guy was Thom Lyons. She had known him all her life, as they were friends, but she liked him a little more.

They had been to dances together before, but this was her Senior year, and she wanted to reveal her feelings to him. Her heart was pounding as Thom didn't have a girlfriend, but he did like one girl from school, as Stella was aware.

Stella kept looking down at her phone, hoping to hear from Thom that he was going to the dance and wanted to take her. Her heart was pounding on a Sunday morning, and she had not seen him in two days.

She combed her blonde hair and then used skin crème for her face as she had acne breakouts at times. Her brownish eyes glared at the mirror as she had finished combing her hair, and then, she was putting on the finishing touches on her face as she glanced down sporadically at her cell.

Stella lived on Water Street, near Bull Moose and McDonald's.

She worked part-time on the weekends at Bull Moose. She was eighteen and did have a license and a car. She drove a 2014 red Nissan

Altima SL. She's had the car for three years, and it was bought for her Birthday. She got her permit and then went for her driver's license and got it the first time.

Her cell remained calm except for Facebook, Twitter, and Instagram notifications. She had profiles on all three platforms. She finished putting crème on her face, and a text came in.

"How about going to the dance with a cool friend?" Stella read it and smiled as there was a smiley face, and she responded: *"How about going to the dance with a smart and cute girl?"* Stella had a wink at the end of the text, and she received a smiley face and a thumbs up.

The dance was on Friday. Stella was excited as she would use this dance to reveal how she felt about him. *"See you tomorrow."* He texted her, and she gave him the thumbs up. Stella wanted to wear something special, *maybe a dress or a dress with scorts...I might have to do some shopping.* Stella thought while deciding to get ready and head out shopping.

***

Thom Lyons smiled as he read the text from Stella. He knew she liked him but was unsure if his feelings were the same. He was with his mother as they came home from Rochester, New Hampshire. He had visited his father, who had been separated from his mother for eight years.

He would see his father every other month as his mother, and he had an agreement. His father would come and visit and vice versa. Thom sat in the passenger seat, glaring at his cell with eager eyes as he was pleased that Stella wanted to go to the dance with him.

"Who's that you're texting? His mother asked with a slight smile.

"It's just Stella, that's all."

"Are you two going to the dance?" His mother smiled and quickly glanced at Thom.

"Yeah, and now, I need to get some new clothes, "he said while looking at his mother and hinting at her about shopping.

"How about sometime this week? Does that work?" His mother asked while driving.

"I have to use the restroom," Thom said, moving a little in his seat and feeling the urge growing.

"Well, there's a rest area up here," his mother suggested, and Thom wanted his mother to pull over, but…

"No, I'm not going to pull over while these cars are speeding by…it's too dangerous!' His mother said with a concerned tone.

"Isn't this the same rest area where the murders happen?" Thom asked with a curious tone.

Thom was a little wary as they approached the rest area exit, and his mother pulled in. She parked the car, looked at Thom, and told him to get moving. Thom glanced at the building and saw two other vehicles, one a truck and the other car.

"Okay, if I get murdered, it's your fault," he said while opening the passenger side door and slowly getting out. He placed his cell in his back pocket while looking around and quickly back at his mother, who gave him a 'let's hurry it up look.'

His mother watched on, and then when Thom walked into the men's room, she turned to her cell and checked her email. The smell had improved since it had been cleaned that morning. Thom saw three urinals and three stalls while there was a closet in the back, and he looked over at the sinks and was anxious to get his business done.

After looking at the stalls and noticing no doors, he used them and got out. He could hear the cars on the highway rushing by, and then he heard a car door slam, and the car there was leaving.

The cloudy sky made the restroom look dim as Thom stood in the last stall; he tried to concentrate and relieve himself but was struggling.

Suddenly, he heard the restroom door open and heard footsteps. Someone had walked in as heavy shoes were heard, and the man was using the urinal as Thom was far over; he tried everything possible to relieve himself, but he was so nervous as, for *one thing, there were no doors on the stalls, and this is where all the killings have taken place…I need to go!* Thom nervously thought as the person was urinating; Thom decided to wait for the person to leave.

The person did their business, washed their hands, and left. Thom quickly forced himself to relieve himself, and he was successful. Thom finished up and quickly washed his hands, and left.

Thom walked fast out of the restroom, made it over to his mother's car, and quickly got in. He sat down, and then Thom turned towards her, and she was sitting up with her tongue ripped out and placed on the steering wheel, and her eyes had been popped by something sharp.

Thom started to scream in the shock of seeing his mother dead, and then, from behind the seat, a man reached around and stabbed Thom in the left eye socket, and Thom quivered, trying to fight off who attacked him and his mother, but he quickly saw the blade piercing his mouth, and Thom cried.

A green ooze streamed from his eye socket, and blood filled his throat as he was choking on his blood; then, he briefly heard slight breathing, and the man placed his thumb on Thom's eye socket, and Thom struggled, but then he was dead. The killer went through the backdoor, slowly walked to his truck, and left. Thom and his mother were found two hours later by a state trooper.

***

Stella heard the news as she arrived at the school the next day, as faculty members and other students were crying. Stella stood by her locker with a picture of her and Thom at Old Orchard Beach with a straight face.

The shock was overwhelming, and Stella had lost the one guy she was in love with.

According to the news and from teachers, a vigil would be held the next day as 'The Rest Area Killer' was to blame. The school sent students home early, and Stella got home and glared at the beautiful dress she had bought for the dance. Stella sat on her bed and cried while a breeze from the open window in Stella's window gently swayed the dress.

Chapter Seventeen

Det. Mitchell was enjoying his time with his grill barbecuing hot dogs and hamburgers. The November air didn't bother him or his grilling outside on the deck. He was having some of his buddies coming over from the force. These buddies worked in various departments within the force.

Det. Mitchell had the food cooked, his buddies were over, and he was enjoying the chilly weather as they wore sweaters and sweatshirts. *Man, what a great day to Cook-out!* He thought to himself as the sun was out. Paul had a picnic table and kept his food in tinfoil containers from Dollar General, which he bought the other day.

The guys helped themselves to the food with chips, dip, and drinks like beer and soda as Paul displayed the food as a buffet. His daughter was at her friend's house for the weekend. It was like a mini-Super Bowl party. Two of his buddies with whom he came from the academy were Giants fans, while the other two were Patriots fans. The two Super Bowl wins by the Giants over the Patriots were always an interesting discussion.

Paul had the big screen TV inside as it was the preshow. The game was Giants at the Patriots.

"So, what is going on with this damn case?!" One of his buddies asked, who worked in Southern Maine.

Paul sat down with the aroma of two hot dogs, potato salad, and a cheeseburger teasing his nostrils. He had a can of Miller Lite, popped the cap, took a drink, and then answered the question.

"As you all know, I can't discuss all the details of an ongoing investigation, but as you've seen in the news, we think the killer drives a black

Ford Ranger," Paul was explaining while taking bites of his freshly cooked hot dog as mustard ran off his lips.

"So, it is true that you think the killer drives a Ford Ranger?" The same friend asked while drinking his beer while the others were looking and eating.

"Absolutely!" Paul said while taking a brief break that he had been eating too fast.

"Shit, man! That's fucked up!" Another friend said.

"It sure is, but the weird thing is, this killer is not just using the rest area; his attacks seemed sporadic. There's no pattern!" Paul was explaining as he continued his feast.

"That's true, man! I take it there are no suspects or anything?" The fourth guy asked before biting into his burger.

"Yeah, it's just no pattern or anything. I hope I can nail this son of bitch!" Paul said with a firm tone.

"Me too, man! Some good people are getting murdered. Is there a task force?" The third friend asked.

Paul knew he didn't want to discuss this case entirely with long-time friends, but *any outside insight could be helpful.* He thought while finishing his hot dog and took another drink of his beer.

"No, there's no task force. It's only me, really, with the exception of Capt. Morse, and that's all. Otherwise, I'm on my own," Paul said before indulging himself in his cheeseburger.

"How about us?!" The first friend suggested, and Paul looked at him, unsure if he was being serious, but Paul liked the idea.

"I would have to pull some strings while talking to Capt. Morse and see what she thinks. Do you think your superiors would be fine with this?"

He asked all of them while drinking his beer and taking another bite of his burger.

All four of them smiled and nodded. Paul smiled, knowing he could use all the help possible but convincing Capt. Morse and the Governor about the idea could be a challenging one.

*****

Ted was outside raking up the remaining leaves with a half-rusted metal rake he found in the garage buried under a couple of shovels and poles used for fences.

Well, this is a beautiful rusted rake. I should have gone to the store and gotten a new one. Ted thought while wet leaves were getting passed the rake as it bent. As a simple chore, Ted thought about going to the store and grabbing a stainless-steel rake from Home Depot was now becoming a complicated one. *Alright, now I'm getting frustrated!*

The family was not home, and he stopped and looked around the landscape. He had hoped to have Shawn around, but since his disappearance has become a fourth nature concern due to the rising murders, Ted lost all hope of finding Shawn.

His eyes were watery as the chilly weather made his eyes hurt, and Ted decided to end his chores and go inside and get warm.

He brought his rusted friend into the garage, which had a rocky bottom, and he smiled, wondering whose idea was to have a rocky bottom, not a typical cement one. *I don't know if the owner who had this done thought it would look more historical than modern, but having a tar driveway and rocky garage... looked stupid!* He thought while grinning and quickly wiped his watery eyes with his L.L. Bean blue cotton jacket. He walked into the house through the garage, which had a side door, and he immediately took his black winter hat and work gloves and placed them on the kitchen counter.

He walked to the fridge, opened it, took out a beer, and started drinking it.

He walked into the living room with his beer in his lap and started watching TV.

His headaches were coming and going. He did have a doctor's appointment tomorrow, as instructed by Terri, as she was worried about him. At one point, she claims she saw him sleepwalking and mumbling words she didn't understand.

I know Terri will be happy with me seeing the docs tomorrow. As these headaches were terrible at times, I too, but now, Terri claims I'm sleepwalking…I love her, but I don't believe in that shit! Ted thought while drinking his beer, and NFL football was on.

Chapter Eighteen

Ted sat in the doctor's office as he was a little nervous. He was at Martin's Point in Portland, on Veranda Street. He had parked in the parking garage not far from the bay. The smell of the bay was soothing.

His eyes gazed at other patients sitting in different sections, such as B7 and D2. He was near the lab test section where patients were tested for blood work such as cholesterol and other infinities.

A headache started again as Ted leaned back into the stiff chair, and he closed his eyes as his cell rested on his lap. "Ted?" A voice was heard behind him, and Ted opened his eyes slightly and quickly got up and said, "Yes?"

"How are you doing today?" The nurse asked while sporting a bun, and she had a white flannel shirt with tan slacks.

"I'm doing ok, but it could be better," Ted added while walking through the door that led into the backroom. They walked down the hallway and approached a room named I5.

"Here we go," the nurse pointed into the room, and Ted walked in, unsure of what to expect and hoping he could get help.

"Please step on the scale as we need to weigh you," the nurse asked while looking over from the computer station to see his weight displayed on the scale, which used digital numbers.

Ted stood tall and made sure his feet were flat. Ted had suffered an injury years ago to his foot, which has never healed appropriately.

"I see you have a slight limp. Is this recent, or did it happen years ago?"

"It happened years ago when I was ten," he said, sitting down and turning his head to face her at the patient station.

"I'm sorry to hear that. How did it happen?" She asked with a curious look.

Ted grew uneasy about the question as it involved his father.

"I choose not to discuss it, please...it's very personal," he said courteously, and the nurse nodded.

"Ok, so. Let's take your blood pressure and check your pulse."

After three minutes of having his right arm wrapped up and squeezed and having his pulse, the nurse got up and said, the doctor will be in shortly to see you," she said with a smile, and Ted thanked her.

He looked around the room, painted white with brown trim. The patient station had a monitor with a computer and an agnomical keyboard. There was a patient bed, which was used for examinations and could rise and go down.

He was surprised he didn't have to redo the forms to go there as he did before. *They must still have all my info from when I came in for a sinus infection a year ago, but that was at a different Martin's Point. So much for Patient confidentiality.* Ted thought as the door opened and the doctor came in.

The doctor was a female, and her name was Dr. Alisha Tallion.

"Hi there. I'm Dr. Tallion. How are you feeling?" She asked while coming in and shaking hands with Ted, who sat with the headache throbbing harshly, but Ted could function as he smiled at the introduction.

"If I were getting better, I wouldn't be here!" He said with a smile, and Dr. Tallion smiled a little but kept it simple.

She was checking his file. "Wow! The last time you were at Martin's Point was a year ago?"

"Yeah, I came in with a bad head cold, which turned out to be a sinus infection."

"So, you are dealing with headaches, correct?" she asked while looking at Ted briefly at the computer.

"Yes. It's going on for a few months now, and it's gotten worse," he said as he didn't want to tell her that the stress was from his son being kidnapped.

"Ok. Let me take a look at you," she said while pointing to the table, and Ted got up and sat on the table.

She checked his throat and neck, then his heart, went behind him, and asked him to take deep breaths. After a couple of minutes, she asked him to step down and sit down.

She walked over to the chair and sat down. She glanced at him and asked him, So, I take it that none of the regular meds are not working?" Ted grew slightly nervous, but he answered as he watched her gently push her hair to the side.

"Yeah, Tylenol and Ibuprofen are not working," he said nervously.

She glanced at him while he was explaining his routine.

"Did you hit your head on anything?"

"Yes, I hit it when we were moving. I hit my head while standing by my car's trunk door, which was not completely open, and I wasn't paying attention."

"Did you ever have headaches like this before?"

"I did it briefly when I was ten, but it stopped six months later! It started again in the last couple of months or so."

"Did you see any doctors?"

"No."

"So, we need to determine if there's anything more serious. I will try and get approval for you to get a cat scan. It depends on your insurance, but I think it will be approved. Can you wait for a few minutes while I check?" She asked, and Ted nodded.

Dr. Tallion got up and left the room.

Ted sat in the chair with a nervous look. His legs were shaking a little as he was relieved that the doctor wanted to do something, but he just hoped it wasn't anything severe but stress. *Oh great! Now they want to check my head and see if everything is still together. Maybe they can find out what the hell is happening also?* Ted thought, and ten minutes passed as he waited patiently for the doctor to return.

The door opened, and the doctor came in and sat down. "Ok, cool. We can do this today at three. How does that sound?" Dr. Tallion asked with an excited tone.

Ted looked at her and said, "Sounds good. Thank you."

Ted would have to go somewhere for three hours and then come back.

"Awesome! See you again in three hours," Dr. Tallion said while Ted got up, guided him to the exit, and explained that he just needed to check in, and they'll show him the way.

"Awesome! See you in three!" She smiled, and Ted thanked her while Ted left and walked downstairs to the parking garage. He got into his vehicle, texted Terri, and told her what was happening.

Chapter Nineteen

Charlie Orson. A 40-year-old from Auburn, Maine, was driving to Old Town to visit his sister, Shawnie, and to meet her fiancé, Cooper.

Charlie drove a 2001 S10 Chevy pickup truck. Charlie had been laid off from Mays Mills in Lewiston. He was currently unemployed as he could not find a suitable job to his liking. *I worked at the mill making paper and things and got the shaft after twenty years! Fuck it! I'll live off the State for a while.* He thought while driving.

Charlie was not a fan of his little sister getting married to a guy she's only known for five months. *This guy and I might not know each other, but we will after today!* He thought while taking a drink of his bottled water.

After coming up to Augusta, Charlie had to piss like a racehorse, but he didn't want to get off the highway. He stopped at the rest area and did his business there. He heard about the murders in the rest area but didn't care.

It was two afternoon, and the urge to go grew more urgent. *My frickin' bladder is going to explode! I should never have had three cups of coffee today and drank all this water.* He thought while driving and adjusting his seating and holding himself.

He could feel his bladder almost letting go, but he held on and saw the rest area was two miles ahead, and he could hold it till then.

He was approaching the rest area with his bladder ready to explode, and he noticed there were two tractor-trailers, two cars, and two pickup trucks.

He parked the car and got out quickly with every stride; he could have sworn he was pissing himself, but he held it. He went into the men's restroom, and there were police yellow ribbons everywhere; it was like a field of ribbons. There were chalk lines on the bathroom floor with a body drawn around them.

He reached the urinal, pulled out his penis, and aimed at it, and *Oh fuck! That feels good. I'm pissing; it feels fucking good!* He stood in place with his penis in his right hand, holding it gently, trying not to spill any on the already urine-smeared floor. He was almost done and suddenly felt someone from behind caressing his buttocks. He retracted his penis into his pants, and he turned quickly and saw a bearded man wearing a shirt that said **John Deere Rules!**

"WHAT THE FUCK ARE YOU DOIN,' YOU FUCKIN' QUEER!?" Charlie started yelling at the bearded stranger. The bearded man said nothing but looked at Charlie with a cold stare, gazing at him all over, and Charlie punched him. The man went down holding his right cheek where Charlie had cocked him well.

The man cried sickeningly, and Charlie couldn't believe it. He looked at the man and felt slightly sorry for him, but that was only for a second. The man got up, holding his right chin with tears rolling down his cheeks, and he gazed at Charlie with a surprised look.

"Why did you hit me?" The bearded man asks while still holding his face, keeping his distance from Charlie.

"You fuckin', ass rubber! You don't know. You think rubbin' a guy's ass while trying to take a piss is cool?!" Charlie asked the man with a raised tone, and he received no response. The bearded man just looked at him, and Charlie had his fist clenched as he wanted to hit the bearded man again.

"You better go, pal!" Charlie said while not moving but grasping his fists tightly.

"I didn't mean to…I just." The bearded man slowly walked towards the entrance, still holding his chin. The bearded man had dry urine on his back; he stared at Charlie while walking back to the entrance and then hurried out of the restroom.

Charlie stared at him and thought, *What the fuck is he looking at!?* Suddenly, Charlie felt someone behind him. He could feel the breathing on his neck, and Charlie immediately grew irritated. *Fuck me! Another perv wants to get frisky with me!* Charlie thought, and he turned around with his fist clenched. Someone was standing behind him; as he looked down and saw feet and there were cowboy boots

As Charlie turned around with his head down and got a shot of the boots that were black with some snakeskin, Charlie felt something piercing him, and a sharp object pierced his groan. Blood streamed from his testicles, and Charlie screamed.

Charlie held his groan while swinging his fist at the attacker, only to hit his leg. The attacker stood and watched Charlie cringe in pain. Charlie looked up and could see the attacker was wearing a hat, almost like a cowboy hat, and he was wearing a half-mask, which was hiding the top half of his face.

"What the fuck is going on…here!?" Charlie said while grabbing his groan, and the pain was overwhelming.

"You're fuckin' dying, bitch! Don't worry, hoss…it won't be long now." The attacker's voice was a little raspy, but it was soft.

"I did nothin' to you…why?" Charlie asked while he was going into shock.

"Stop thinkin', Cunt! JUST DIE!!" The attacker said while yelling, but his body motion was calm.

Charlie tried to move while feeling the wetness and the pain as he tried to crawl, but he was dying.

The attacker walked around him towards the entrance, but he wasn't heading for the entrance; he blocked Charlie from exiting. The attacker knelt by Charlie's head like he was blessing him and drew a cross on

Charlie's forehead, but that wasn't The attacker's intention. The attacker gripped both sides of Charlie's head and jerked it quickly to the right, and his neck *snapped!* Charlie's body twitched a couple of times.

The attacker stood up while taking his foot and gently touching Charlie's face, admiring his work. As he looked at Charlie, the attacker chuckled a little, and he slowly turned towards the exit and walked out. Charlie's lifeless eyes, with his blood-soaked clothes, gazed into the unknown darkness known as death...

Chapter Twenty

Reporters again swarmed the rest area as another body was found. Det. Mitchell looked at the man lying on the floor with his lifeless gaze. *Well, that look never loses its creepiness.* Det. Mitchell thought while a little freaked out by the eyes staring in his direction.

"What happened here?" Capt. Morse walked into the men's restroom and was slightly overwhelmed by the piss and blood odor.

"This is different. He snapped the victim's neck after stabbing him in the groan area," Det. Mitchell was explaining as he was pointing, and Capt. Morse observed.

"So, you think this is the 'Rest Area Killer'?" She asked with a curious look while looking at Det. Mitchell.

"Absolutely!"

"We have an FBI agent coming in who does profiles on serial killers. The Governor is bringing him in," Capt. Morse said while seeing Det. Mitchell, in her statement, did not truly overjoy Mitchell.

"FBI?! Crap! He's going to want to take the case over, and I'll be taking orders from him! I don't like it!" Det. Mitchell said firmly while getting up after kneeling and looking down at the victim.

"We need help, Paul! We have no idea who this killer is! Maine has a serial killer that has a thing for this rest area, and we need to know why?" Capt. Morse explained, and Det. Mitchell listened, and he understood, but he didn't like it.

"I was hoping we would get someone from within the state, who has some kind of expertise," Paul explained as he understood what Capt. Morse was saying, but he was worried that his case...would no longer be *his* case.

"Listen, I know you're unhappy with the decision, but we *need help,* Paul! What choice do we have? We're dealing with someone two steps ahead of us," Capt. Morse said firmly, standing with Det. Mitchell.

Det. Mitchell looked at her with disagreement.

"So, why do you think he snapped his neck?" Capt. Morse refocused on the victim, and Det Mitchell followed her lead.

"I don't think he was dying quickly. I think that he was crawling, and the killer stopped him from trying to exit, and then he grew frustrated and snapped his neck. You see how he's positioned?" Det. Mitchell was showing his conclusion, and Capt. Morse nodded.

"We need to close this rest area permanently!" Det. Mitchell said firmly, and Capt. Morse turned and rolled her eyes as she was facing the exit and agreed with Det. Mitchell, but it was out of her control. "You have to understand, Paul. I don't have the control, and I know that the Governor and the Commissioner won't go for it, either. I've already tried." Capt. Morse said with a frustrated tone.

"Well, we need seventy-two hours to thoroughly check for fingerprints, urine samples, and anything we can find to identify this killer," Det. Mitchell was asking.

"CSI is going to love you after all of this. I'm sure they'll love digging around in this shit hole and digging up some guy's week-old sperm," Capt. Morse stated while making her way to the exit.

"I'm sure they will," Det. Mitchell said with a smirk, and he continued with his investigation while waiting for the CSI to show up. Capt. Morse went outside and answered questions from the pressing reporters.

***

Terri glanced at the TV in the breakroom and was in disbelief about the horrific killings.

All those people are getting killed, and my son, Shawn, is missing after all these months...the police are useless! She thought while eating a chicken sandwich she made this morning.

Terri was drinking bottled water with her sandwich, and she had sliced carrots in a medium size baggie. She also had a thousand island dressing, where she would dip her carrots into. For her, it was an indulging snack.

"Hi, Terri. How're things?" One of the employees came in, and she saw Terri eating her lunch.

"I'm ok. How about you, Karen?"

"Same stuff every day, but nothing changes," Karen said while walking to the fridge and taking out her plastic bag filled with her lunch.

"You don't mind if I sit with you?" Karen asked while holding her bag of lunch, and Terri nodded.

Karen sat at the circled table with red and white squares engraved in it, and Karen took out her lunch and placed it neatly on the table.

Terri briefly watched her unload her lunch, which was like a full meal, as Karen had four baked chicken legs, a container with mashed potatoes, a brownie, and a bottle of Coke.

"Talk about a full meal," Terri said with a slight smile as she was surprised to see such a meal at lunchtime.

Karen smiled and said, "Yeah, I love leftovers. My husband doesn't care for them, but that's him, not me!" Karen smiled and decided to warm up her chicken and mashed potatoes.

Karen placed the chicken on a plate that was in the cabinet. She quickly washed it, placed her chicken on it, and put it into the microwave for two minutes.

"Any word about your son?" Karen asked, as she was one of the employees that knew what happened to Terri and her family.

Terri was quiet at first as she was focused on her lunch and didn't want to think about Shawn.

"Everything is still the same," she murmured, and Karen looked at her with concerned eyes and felt that maybe she shouldn't be asking.

"I'm sorry for asking...my bad!" Karen said with a concerned tone.

"No biggie. As I said, everything is still the same."

Karen finished warming up her food, walked to the table with a full plate, and brought her silverware.

"You did bring everything, didn't you?" Terri asked with a slight smile; she was a little surprised as she watched Karen sit down, adjust her lengthy hair, and indulge in her lunch.

Terri didn't say much as she thought about Shawn, hoping he was still alive. *My son has to be still alive....he has to be.* She thought with her eyes watery and decided to end her lunch and return to work. She said goodbye to Karen, who had mashed potatoes with butter dripping from her lips.

Chapter Twenty-One

Det. Mitchell instructed CSI to take samples of the entire interior of the restroom. He received some frowns, except for Nathan, the lead inspector. He had known Paul for three years and had a typical business relationship with him.

"You just want to see our work, don't you?" He asked with a smirk as Det. Mitchell stood outside, and Nathan stood beside him, watching his workers scrap up some nasty shit.

"Any ideas on what the hell is going on here?" Nathan asked while taking out a cig from his jacket pocket and lit it. Det. Mitchell looked at him while seeing the reporters surrounding the rest area like a swarm of yellow jackets.

"This killer uses this rest area as the main killing ground, but he did kill elsewhere. Capt. Morse has a serial killer profilist from the FBI coming, and he might be able to help us out."

"I'm just kinda surprised that there's no task force or anything on this matter," Nathan said while puffing.

"The only thing about having a task force; is too many chefs in the kitchen, and things can get messy. Look at some of the killings in the past, such as Zodiac, Bundy, Gacy, and The Hillside Strangler. They had a task force, but some didn't work out."

"Well, shit, man! They never caught Zodiac, though...I think that case is still open," Nathan said, and Paul looked at him and said, "It sure is."

"So, you're the only one on this case?" Nathan asked with a curious tone.

"Well, Capt. Morse is helping and you as well, mister." Paul smiled and gently tapped Nathan's arm, who took another puff.

"Yeap! The highlights of my job...scraping cum and piss off a dirty cement floor, and my career is going nowhere," Nathan took a puff while he had to get back inside and finish his work.

"So, you guys think this is, 'The Rest Area Killer?'" While looking at Paul, Nathan asked, and Paul replied with a "Yes."

"At least it's kinda creepy but memorable," Nathan said, throwing his butt to the ground and heading inside.

Det. Mitchell scanned the reporters as; also, there was a gathering crowd. Based on his research, such as 'Son Of Sam.' Berkowitz would hang around the scene and watch the police work, almost indulging and enjoying his handy work. Paul thought while walking a little.

He walked where the line of people started and scanned everyone from old to young. *Who the fuck was this guy, and why he is doing this?* Det. Mitchell looked for anyone who might seem' curious' about the crime scene.

You did have your typical weirdos who come to the station and confess they were the killer, but they weren't. They were just into the fame and getting their little ugly face all over the news. Det. Mitchell went to his car, but his eyes remained on the swarm of people.

***

"Honey, are you ok?" Terri asked Ted, lying on the sofa with an ice pack on his head and looking pale. Terri walked up to him and took his temp.

"Wow! You feel warm. Are you ok?" She asked with a concerned look.

"I feel like shit!" He muttered, unable to speak normally as it would bother his headache.

"Did you ever go to the doctor?"

"I did. I was scheduled for a cat scan, but they ended up canceling due to a schedule conflict, and I'm just waiting for them to call me back," he said while his head was tilted; the ice was packed was held by his right hand.

"I can't believe they canceled last second. You had waited all day, right?"

"Yeah, it was down to the last half hour, and I came back to the office to check in, and they told me they had to cancel," Ted said while talking out loud was hurting.

Terri looked on with a concerned look. "Maybe you should go to the hospital and get looked at," She suggested, and Ted nodded 'no.'

She didn't want to argue with him, but based on his current health status, she decided to let him be.

"Well, try to get some rest. I love you." She walked over and gently kissed his forehead. The warmness of his forehead warmed her lips upon touching. She was worried about him.

"Luv you, too!" He murmured, and Terri walked out of the living room while Ted layed on the sofa, almost paralyzed from the lousy headache. While watching programming, he had the TV remote in his left hand, but the volume was meager.

His eyes grew wary and tired. Ted fell asleep with the ice pack on his head but would eventfully fall off due to his body shifting during sleep.

Chapter Twenty-Two

Det. Mitchell was in his office, looking at the crime scenes' photos taken and waiting for Sgt. Williams to come in and meet with him. Det. Mitchell had looked at his file from the Androscoggin County Sheriff's office, and Paul felt Sgt. Vic Williams would be an excellent addition to his 'one-man team.'

A knock at his door, and Det. Mitchell said, "Come in."

Walking in was Sgt. Williams, who was wearing his sheriff's uniform, and Det. Mitchell looked up at him with a firm look.

"Hello, Detective, I'm Det. Mitchell. I'm the head investigator on 'The Rest Area Killer' case. Do you know why you're here?" Det. Mitchell sat in his chair and looked at the nervous sergeant with a firm look.

"Sir, I believe you need some help. I believe you're asking my help because you don't want any outside parties coming in," Sgt. Williams said while standing straight up and showing good posture.

Det. Mitchell got up from his chair and walked over to Sgt. Williams, staring at him face-to-face. Sgt. Williams could feel the uneasiness within the office.

"Is there a problem, sir?" Sgt. Williams asked with a slightly nervous tone.

"No. I'm the one that requested you. I'm looking for someone from this beautiful state with expertise in serial killers. Now, keep in mind Capt. Morse is having an FBI profilist come in, but I have the authority to have some help from inside." Det. Mitchell stated as it was partially true, but he never asked Capt. Morse for permission to have help from a county sheriff.

Sgt. Williams stood still with a firm posture as his hair was neatly combed and clean-shaven. He was in good shape as he worked out and didn't drink. Paul liked the fact he was self-disciplined and took his job seriously.

"So, answer me this question, Sargeant. Why the sheriff's department? How come you didn't try to become a trooper?" Det. Mitchell was curious as Paul sat on his desk's edge, waiting for Vic to respond.

"Sir, I did, but they felt I was not 'firm enough' to be a trooper," he explained.

Det. Mitchell had a confused face and asked, "When did this happen? And who is the person that told you this?" Det. Mitchell asked with a curious tone.

"Sir, it was eight years ago, and I believe it was Capt. Hill. He told me I was not 'firm enough to be a trooper.' So, I started working out and keeping myself on a disciplined schedule," Sgt. Williams explained, and Det. Mitchell nodded.

"I remember Capt. Hill. He was not fond of me when I was a trooper, but Sargeant, that was then, and this is now. Capt. Morse is a cool captain," Det. Mitchell said with a smile, and Sgt. Williams smiled a little.

"Welcome to 'The Rest Area Killer' task force," Det. Mitchell said, extending his hand, and Sgt. Williams replied, "Thank you, sir."

Of course, later on...Paul would have to explain his action to Capt. Morse.

***

Ted was in his office working on some forms. As he was working, he got word that the bank was rumored to be bought out by another bank. Other employees had been speculating as Ted remained calm and felt it was just a rumor. *I understand their job concerns if a possible merger or a bank is financially in trouble. We need to remain calm.* He thought while shifting through files.

"Hey Ted, can we talk?" A voice was heard at the door and Ted turned around and it was his manager.

Ted stopped doing what he was doing, and his manager sat down.

"What's happening, Martin?" Ted asked while leaning forward in his chair and giving his manager full attention.

Martin sat with his shirt tied gently neat, had blonde highlights, and his goatee was groomed.

"I'm not sure if you're aware of it, but we are dealing with some financial problems."

Ted glanced at Martin, feeling a slight uneasiness within him.

"I've heard rumors, that's all," Ted said while trying to remain calm and not seem nervous.

"Well, another institution is looking to help us out, but there will probably be some cuts," Martin said with a remorseful tone.

Ted leaned forward, and the nervousness was full frontal.

"Martin, what's going on?" Ted asked while trying to remain calm.

"In two weeks, you, I, and ten other employees will no longer be working here...we'll be unemployed."

Ted's eyes widened, and rage started to build within.

"You gotta be fuckin' kiddin' me! First, I lost my son, dealing with these dam headaches, and now, I'm losing my job...?!" Ted stood up, and Martin sat, remaining calm and cordial.

"Ted, I'm sorry. I'm losing my job too!" Martin said while standing up, trying to justify what was happening. Ted started to pace a little as he glanced at the family photos on his desk and out of his office, seeing the streets and small gas station.

"I can't lose my job, Martin! My family and I moved here!" Ted's voice echoed loudly as the other employees could hear Ted's rage.

"Ted, please be calm. I'm losing my job as well as ten other employees. Some have already given their notices while others are waiting to reapply with the new institution," Martin explained, trying to calm Ted, who was full of rage and immediately started kicking his desk and the wall.

"Oh, FUCK IT! WHAT DO I CARE!? I'M LOSIN' MY DAMN JOB, MARTIN!" Ted yelled, and Martin stood still, staring at Ted, and he glanced down and decided to leave Ted's office. He left while closing the door. Ted's face was red and full of rage; Ted paced while feeling angry.

After five minutes, Ted started to calm down and started to focus. His main concern was, *how will I explain this to Terri? I know she has an excellent job working at the bank, but we moved here because of me...she was super happy working from home...How will I explain and look at her with my pride destroyed..?*

Ted sat back in his chair as his eyes were watery, and his headache was nothing but an echo. At this point, nothing affected him. He decided to continue to calm down, and instead of working, he decided to go online and do some job hunting. *The fuckin' bastards are going to fire me...well, FUCK THEM! I'll do some job searching, and then, maybe on my last day, I'll punch Martin in the fuckin' face!* Ted angrily thought and felt Martin was responsible; even though he told Ted he was losing his job, Ted didn't believe him.

Ted finished his day by taking longer breaks and barely working...

Chapter Twenty-Three

Janice and Wally Coleman had been retired for five years. Janice had been a nurse at Central Maine Medical Center, while Wally worked for Eastland Shoe in Freeport, which is now closed and is a public parking area. Gardening was their thing while taking walks along the Kennebec River.

Their charming garden homed tomatoes, carrots, and peas.

Both were 67 years old and enjoying their retirement, even though Janice missed working at the hospital rather than watching Wally take quick naps throughout the day.

She took up gardening to ease her sanity and keep herself from killing Wally and his enjoyment of toy trains and construction vehicles. Not the plastic ones, but the metal ones used to be made to beat on but would rust during the winter months if left outside all winter.

"Wally, what are you doing in the woods?" She yelled while hanging up clothes.

"Nothing," He said.

She had wondered if he was building a fort out there and pretending he was a kid again.

"I found something," He yelled to get her attention.

"What is it?" She shouted, rolling her eyes.

"There's a shack out here." Janice stopped quickly and thought of all the times he had gone out there, and now there was a shack out there… *How?* She thought.

She waited for him to say more, but he didn't. He was silent. Immediate concern grew within her as she walked to the woods near her clothesline, and she was looking into the thickly wooded area and saw nothing.

There was no shack of any kind in the woods. She figured that Wally had ventured a little deeper. He yelled for her after seeing the shack and wanted her to come out.

"Alright, I'm on my way," she shouted while Wally stood on the edge of the woods, looking in and then looking back at Janice on her progress of walking to him.

As she walked on dried leaves and branches, the weather was a little chilly, but she hung clothes until it was freezing; then, she used the dryer.

Wearing just sneakers and a sweater, she reached the edge of the woods, but Wally was gone!

"Wally, where are you?" She yelled while looking around, hoping to catch a glimpse of him. No response.

"Wally, where are you?" she asked loudly while breaking branches along the way; she was going into the woods hoping to see him.

"Over here." A soft voice from the side of her. She looked around and saw Wally standing in front of a metal shack.

The shack was a bit rusty, plain gray, with some scratches and a few dents.

"I've been looking for you. I was concerned. What the hell were you doing out here?" She asked, staring at Wally's pale face. He was mumbling, and he just stared at her and kept mumbling.

By the reaction on his face. He'd seen a ghost, but these woods were reported to be haunted or anything like that.

"Wally, what the matter?" She asked with a concerned tone. No reaction. Just the same. *Something has scared the shit out of Wally, and I wish I knew what it was, that silly bastard!* Janice thought while walking to him as he stared at the shack with a stunning look.

Wally turned to her slowly, and he kept mumbling, "I saw-I saw…a boy in there." His hands were on his face, and suddenly, Janice got a bad feeling. She asked, "What do you mean, Wally?" She said while looking at him, knowing something was wrong.

Janice saw the shack, and she wondered what was inside the shack that would get Wally into such a weird state. She went inside the shack and saw for herself what was in there that scared the hell of Wally.

"Wally, I'm going inside the shack to see what is happening." She said bluntly. No reaction, just mumbling from Wally. Her heart beat a little faster, and even though it was already beating fast while looking for Wally, she was very nervous and anxious.

Stepping on broken tree limbs and branches. She was making her way slowly toward the shack, and she *felt* something was in there, but she was trying to prepare herself for the worse or whatever was in there.

She approached the shack, and the door was half-open, just enough to walk through and go inside. *Why am I doing this? I can't believe this shack is here. I hope there is nothing in here.* She prayed a little, hoping it would help deal with whatever was in there.

She looked into the shack and saw the opening had cobwebs everywhere as the shack had been there long, but it seemed it had been moved a little. Janice couldn't believe what she was doing, "Oh Lord, don't let me get into something bad," She said rapidly out loud as she looked inside and saw webs, a couple of boxes, and something in the back.

There was a shift in the back, and Janice stood frozen with fear, and suddenly, it was moving, and it slowly crawled on the wooden floor covered with old tree limbs, and there were food crumbs everywhere and, *Gotta move! Gotta move!* She thought over and over, and then a raspy voice was heard, "Please help me."

The voice was faint and thin. Janice heard the sound, and she looked into the corner of the shack, which was filled with darkness and slowly the shifting, was coming closer, and then she saw it was…A boy!

Chapter Twenty-Four

The state police were called to a West Gardiner home where a small boy was found in a shack hidden in the woods, and there was speculation about what happened to the boy and who he was. The local publication had posted an online article.

The findings indicate new things for some lonely parents who had lost their son, but who was the boy? Local news found out and posted the article. Wally and Janice were locally famous, and they were asked hard questions, and speculation spread through the state. Some of it leaked into nearby states, such as New Hampshire, Massachusetts, and Vermont. Det. Mitchell was called to West Gardiner, and the local officials questioned Wally and Janice, who knew the couple and were waiting for Det. Mitchell to arrive. Det Mitchell arrived on the scene with the thoughts on his mind thinking this had nothing to do with the rest area killings, so when he arrived, he noticed an old couple in tears, and some of the local police and state police were smiling tearfully.

Are state Troopers crying? What the hell is going on…? Standing in front of Det. Mitchell wearing old clothes, dehydrated and very pale, and had been missing for weeks, Shawn. Det. Mitchell stood in his place, glaring down at the young child and seeing the innocence dwindle within.

Det. Mitchell looked at Shawn, and he fought to hold back watery eyes.

"Hey, son, are you ok?" Paul asked the frightened boy.

Shawn could not speak. He nodded a little, and Paul placed his right hand on his shoulder and told him, "Everything will be alright, son." The remorseful tone slightly soothed Shawn's heightened awareness.

Det. Mitchell recognized him from the photos, as did others. The paramedics gave him a small IV, but they could barely do it.

"We need to get him to the hospital," a paramedic said, and Det. Mitchell nodded.

Det. Mitchell stood there by the house where the paramedics had brought him to. Shawn was alive from the shack, and he couldn't believe that after all these weeks, he was alive! He wanted to ask Shawn questions, but Shawn's family had to be notified before anything else occurred. *I cannot believe this kid is alive!... Someone had kept him fed and given him some liquids, but the shack smelled like a dumpster.*

Det. Mitchell knew there would be such a great relief to the family, considering that Shawn had been missing for months, and somehow he survived, but Det. Mitchell suspects that whoever kidnapped Shawn is still at large, and the question remains…*was 'The Rest Area Killer' associated with the kidnapping of Shawn? It all started with the boy's disappearance, but why was Shawn spared? Maybe this killer has a heart for kids or something?* Det. Mitchell thought while seeing Shawn being carried out on the stretcher; the paramedics were with him, ensuring he was given enough fluids.

Det. Mitchell returned to the shack and saw buckets filled with urine and waste. *Fuck me! This poor kid...*Paul tearfully thought as he never saw anything like this.

Even with the cold air, the shack was exerting an acrid smell.

Det. Mitchell walked over to Janice and Wally and started to interview them.

"Who found the boy first?"

"It was me, sir," Wally said with tears running down his cheeks.

"So, did you ask or tell your wife to come out?" Det. Mitchell asked with a firm tone.

"Yes, sir. He asked me to come out, and I did." Janice said.

"Was there anyone else around upon the discovery?"

"No, sir. We saw no one else," Wally said while trembling as he watched Shawn and the ambulance leave.

"I opened the door, and there in the back was the boy," Janice said with surprised eyes.

"Is the shack located directly on your land?" Det. Mitchell asked while jotting down notes.

"It's actually on edge, but this was the first time I had come this far," Wall explained.

"What made you come out this far, then?" Det. Mitchell asked.

"Around this time, before the cold hits, we sometimes find blueberries, and I pick them and give them to Janice to make me pie," Wally trembled, scared that the detective would see him as a suspect.

Det. Mitchell asked the couple to show him where Wally would pick blueberries, and Wally got up off a log and started walking. Det. Mitchell asked Janice to stay where she was, and she nodded.

Wally guided Det. Mitchell and ahead of them, Det. Mitchell bushes of blueberries, and he stopped and looked over to see the shack, but it was attractive to him how a shack could be placed here.

"Was that shack always there?"

"No, there was nothing there last year, but somehow, it was placed there, and as I said, I didn't know until I saw it," Wally said with a nervous tone, and Det. Mitchell told him calmly to relax. *Don't worry, old timer...I'm not going to arrest you for discovering the boy.* Paul thought, and then he walked around while Wally watched.

Det. Mitchell walked over to the part of the woods where there was a snowmobile trail and scanned it. He knelt and touched the cold ground and could feel the ground getting frost a little.

"That's it for now, sir. Thank you!" Det. Mitchell said to Wally and headed back to where Janice was. The trail led to where the shack was, as Det. Mitchell walked around shrubs and looked down, hoping to see something that indicated something.

Det. Mitchell saw no big tire tracks; *even though the ground was almost brutal, there would have been some kind of impression.* Det. Mitchell thought while he walked a little on the trail, he walked into a field, and then he noticed he could hear lots of cars, but he didn't know where it was coming from.

He turned around and decided to head back to the shack, but suddenly, he looked ahead and could see the shack, and there was a number and a letter on the side of the shack.

He took out his notepad and wrote the info down. The info was **A3.** *Shit, that's some kind of identification!?* Det. Mitchell thought while he decided to head back and check in with the CSI and asked them to look for any tire tracks.

Chapter Twenty-Five

Ted was home, sleeping in his recliner, and the rest of the family was at a friend's house.

The phone was ringing, and Ted thought he was dreaming, but then he woke up, and he came to his senses and realized the phone ringing was no dream. He got up and out of his recliner too quickly and suddenly had some dizziness, but it quickly disappeared.

He was still disoriented, finally realizing where the ringing was coming from, and he picked it up.

"Hello there. Is Mr. Patterson there?" A soft-spoken female voice asked.

"This is. May I ask who's speaking?" Ted asked while his heart was beating fast.

"Hi. Mr. Patterson, this is Lt. Dickens from the Augusta Police Department, and I'm calling about your son, Shawn. We found, and he's alive!" Lt. Dickens said excitedly.

"What!?" Ted asked confusingly.

"Sir, your son has been found. And he's alive!" Lt. Dickens said once again. Ted stared at the kitchen, and his jaw dropped! Suddenly, he got a little light-headed again. He almost had a panic attack, but he breathed calmly, and everything was getting better now.

"My boy, Shawn, is found alive?" Ted asked the soft-spoken lieutenant.

"Yes, sir. He's alive!" Lt. Dickens said the third time as Ted was in shock.

Ted just looked upon the kitchen now, and he imagined how it was possible to hear a soft voice over the phone telling him that his son,

Shawn was alive! *They found my boy! They found my boy! I can't believe it. They found my boy!*

"Sir? Are you still there?" Lt. Dickens asked

"Yes. I'm still here. I can't believe it. You found my boy!"

"Yes, sir. We did." Lt. Dickens confirmed it.

Ted stood in place with the phone in his right hand up to his ear, and his left hand covered his mouth as he was trying to calm down, and Lt. Dickens, at first, thought he had a heart attack, but with the experience, she knew he was ecstatic!

"Sir? Are you ok?" She asked once more while waiting for a response from the heavy-breathing and excited father.

"I'm all right," He answered softly.

"Good, sir. It would help if you came to Maine General Hospital in Augusta, where he's being transferred. We found him in West Gardiner in a shack near an elderly couple's home." She said.

Ted couldn't believe it. *They found Shawn! My Boy! The only son I have. Terri will be ecstatic!* Ted cried.

"Sir? Are you all right?" The Lieutenant asked.

"I find, thanks." Ted was short while crying.

Lt. Dickens continued her conversation, and then she ended with a…. "You're welcome." She said and hung up.

As Ted put the phone down, he imagined seeing Shawn in an old shack with things crawling around him like spiders, bugs, and everything else living in old and dark places. Tears rolled down his pale cheeks.

He gently went to the floor while holding the phone in his trembling hand.

"Honey? Are you all right?" Terri asked while looking down at him with her sweetness of a face, and her smile of concern filled Ted's face with a huge smile, and he only realized the phone call he received was real and was not part of a dream.

"You were asleep. How come you were asleep on the floor, Ted?" She asked with concern.

"They called! They called!" Ted said excitedly.

"Who called, honey?" She looked down at him while he slowly got up, and there was an enormous smile on his face, almost a mile long.

"They called! The police called! They found Shawn! And he's alive!" He said while trying to hug her and preparing for her to drop to her feet.

"They found Shawn!" She screamed, and they embraced, and for a time, they embraced for something positive, and they embraced for minutes while they both cried.

The kids came into the house after they were out playing, and Laurie was behind them after they all went shopping, and Laurie saw something in her parents.'

Ted and Terri told the kids as they did a little group hug, and all cried. The family was almost reunited, except without Shawn, but soon he'll be with them.

"We have to go to Maine General. That's where he is." Ted said while looking at his family.

"Well. We'd better get moving." Terri suggested.

They gathered their things, Ted changed his clothes, and they all went outside and got into their vehicle and were on their way to Maine General in Augusta.

Chapter Twenty-Six

Sue Redding was working at the bank, covering for Ted's duties, knowing he had been going through a lot. She had been the Assistant Manager for five years and was unsure if she was losing her job also.

Sue was 44 and unmarried but engaged to a 40-year-old retail sales manager at Best Buy in South Portland. Ted called her on his cell phone about the good news, and she was ecstatic for the family. *I'm glad everything is well. I'm glad they found Shawn. I know it was tearing apart that family.* Sue thought while having watery eyes and was relieved about the good news.

The bank was closed, and the rest of the tellers had left as Sue was finishing up, and she was depositing the money into the safe, and *Best Security* will be here on Monday.

All the doors were locked, and she ensured everything was secured for the cleaners when they came in tonight. The bathrooms need to be cleaned because the cleaning company never came on Friday night, and… *fricking gross!* Sue stared at the bathroom and couldn't believe some people were just slobs! Her thoughts were… *Why?*

She cleaned the bathroom a little or just enough for the cleaning crew wouldn't get upset.

She flushed the toilets as two were not flushed. *This is friggin' gross!* She thought with disgust.

After cleaning up, Sue went to the back where her things were, and she was on her way out, and something inside her told her that she had forgotten something. *The safe! Oh, sure, let's keep the safe open and let the underpaid workers take it because it's well deserved.* Trash-talking the cleaning crew was something she never did or hopefully never will. Face-to-face confrontations were not her specialty, but if she was angry enough, *watch out…Dragon Lady in da' house!* Sue locked up the safe, and then she walked towards the front and noticed a man wearing a blue polo shirt; he was wearing plain sunglasses with blonde hair, and he was standing by the front entrance, and he just stood there looking at Sue, and she realized something wasn't right.

Sue was halfway between the front door and the main entrance; she was in the mini lobby between the doors, and they felt this 'someone' stopping by for a reason standing in her direction of the exit. She stopped in her footsteps and waved at the gentleman, but there was no response.

She felt uneasy. *Who is this guy? Fucker, you better think twice about doing something here!*

"Sir? The bank is closed. I can't help you! Please go!" She yelled at him while waving her right arm to go away, but the man silently stood there, motionless.

She went back inside and called the police. As she turned, the man walked away to the left of her. She watched him, and he was striding with a few glimpses at her. Then, he walked away to the left side and was out of sight.

Sue felt a nervousness rising to the occasion, and she stopped by the front door; she felt something was up, and all she thought of was one of these scenes from horror movies; *I don't want to be one stupid teenage girl wondering if the killer was still and to go outside then and BOOM! You're dead! No thanks! I'll call the police!* Sue thought while uneasiness grew.

Sue got on one of the business phones to call the police, but suddenly she saw the man by the drive-thru window, and he stood there motionless, and he said nothing but stare. The polo shirt the man was wearing was ironed smoothly as if the man wanted to look good for Sue.

Sue held the phone to her right heart and glanced back at the man. Waiting for him to do something would give her a reason to call. Regardless of how strange the man might be; you cannot call the police expecting them to do something unless the person had done something to either provoke or come close of doing something deviously.

Sue wasn't sure who the man was, but he gave Sue the creeps. As she watched him staring at her from the drive-thru window, she noticed that he was smiling at her and his teeth were pure yellow as if he had never brushed his entire life, but then the smile slowly turned into a smirk, and then it dissolved into an authentic expression.

Sue got on the phone and dialed 9-1-1, and the operator answered, and then the man was gone. Sue hung up the phone and ran to the drive-th-ru window to see if the man was still there but hiding. *Running with heels was difficult, especially if you broke your leg or sprang your ankle.*

Sue was running, but she sprinted towards the main door where her car awaited her in the parking lot and then as she was running, the phone turned to her left, and she went for it and hoped for the best. *No doubt! It was the police! I must get to my car and get out here. Got to get my keys out and use them as a weapon.* The sudden rush out and running to her car was erratic as she wanted to leave.

Sue was by the front door, her car was in view, and she held her keys between her fingers as individual spikes or knuckles, and she held them ready to strike, so she unlocked the front door cautiously while constantly looking around for the man that had crept on her. The door opened hard, and she was finally outside and then she turned to lock the door, and suddenly…from behind, she felt someone behind her.

A gentle hand landed softly on her shoulder, and she suddenly felt fear, then she told herself she wouldn't become a victim, and she turned quickly and…It was one of the tellers' of the bank.

"Sue. Are you ok?" Phil asked while looking at Sue with urgency.

"I'm ok. Thanks. What are you doing back here, Phil?" Sue was look-ing at him, feeling safe and knowing whoever the man was or what he was planning to do, he was gone!

"I forgot my cell phone." His mustache was half-trimmed with a few whiskers that dangled near his lips.

"Oh, I see." She noticed he needed to trim his mustache but decided not to say anything.

Phil went inside and walked behind the counter where tellers would work and assist customers with their accounts and finances.

He found his cell phone on the side of his little counter with a coffee stain that had dried and had been neglected by the cleaning crew. Phil left the bank feeling relieved that he had found his cell, heading out and trying to enjoy his boring weekend. He played golf on Saturday afternoon and then went to the movies with his cheating girlfriend of two years, Hilda.

Sue closed the bank with the keys jingling, and she watched Phil leaving and then she walked out to her car; which was roasting in the summer air, and her was looking at the car and realized," "Get in the fuckin' car, you cunt!" A voice from behind her startled her, and she remembered her keys were still positioned in her knuckles like brass knuckles.

"What do you want?" She asked carefully, feeling the urge to hit the man behind her.

"The money in the bank, you cunt!" His voice drove a deep spark from within her, and hated the word *cunt! You never call a woman that! Ever! You stupid fuck!* She felt his hands on her shoulder as if he had something in his other hand, but what?

She stood in place like she was frozen or if she was a statue; something captured in time. She didn't want to be captured…at all! She had hoped that Phil or one teller would return or a customer, but no one was around for some reason.

She felt she had a sign on; however, *Stay away! I'm being robbed! Thanks!*

"C'mon bitch, give it to me!" The stranger said with anger building in his tone.

"What are you asking?" She asked, trying to keep her composure.

"You know what I want!" He said impatiently.

She was trying to figure out what he wanted, but he wasn't asking the right question, or she was misinterpreting what he wanted.

"Don't fuck around, you cunt!" He retorted, and she felt he was going to do something quickly, and she suddenly felt a sharp prick behind her neck and then…She said, "How much do you want?" She asked while closing her eyes, hoping the stranger wanted that.

"Give me all the fucking money and even more than that!" The stranger was angry, and the tip of his blade dug a little into Sue's neck, and she quenched her eyes a little, thinking he would stick her at any moment.

"Let me get my keys out, and I'll.."

"No fuckin' tricks, you bitch!" He said to her while holding her close to him tightly. Sue got out her keys, which had dropped into her purse, after she felt the hands from behind.

The keys jingled a little, and the stranger chuckled with ease, and she felt his grip loosened, and she turned the keys into her fingers like spikes, and then at the right moment, she waited, she turned around, and then… She struck the stranger across the nose, and he went down to the ground knocking the sunglasses off his face and revealing the man.

The keys remained within her fingers, and she held the keys with her right hand like, and she held it like it was an iron fist.

"Come on, you son of a bitch!" She was yelling at him, feeling the adrenaline, and he looked at her, and suddenly she saw his eyes filled with fear, and then he put out his hands begging her not to hurt him while blood rushed out of his nose like a small stream and she said, "Get up, you fuck!" She yelled at him once more, and then the stranger got up quickly while looking at her, and he ran off, but he didn't get far as the police arrived and the police halted the stranger as they saw the knife in his hands.

Her heart was beating a thousand times, feeling pure fear and then turning it into pure adrenaline, and she couldn't believe what she had done.

She gathered her composure, and two police officers exited their squad car and arrested the man. After the suspect was in custody, they walked over to Sue, who was shaken up, gathered her thoughts, and told them what had happened.

"I thought I had hung up the phone," she said while trying to calm down.

"The number that showed up, the caller ID showed it was from this location," one of the officers explained. Sue was relieved, but she was glad she was leaving. Sue sat with the police and asked if that was the killer from the rest area, and they nodded 'no.' Det. Mitchell arrived and ensured it wasn't, but the killings have been a factor in surrounding communities. He explained, and she was somewhat relieved. Hours later, they tracked down the attacker, and he was arrested. He had been stalking Sue for quite some time.

Chapter Twenty-Seven

Shawn was in the emergency room at Maine General Hospital in Augusta.

Doctors and nurses checked him for bruises and other things such as knife marks, sexual abuse, and malnutrition.

Shawn was lying down on the gurney, tired and scared, and he wanted his parents. His face was pale with bloodshot eyes, and he had lost some weight as he was very frail.

The doctor in charge looked at him and could see Shawn struggling to remain awake as he was dehydrated and would take a day or two with fluids to have him almost recovered. *Poor kid...*The doctor thought while he examined him.

"Alright, we need to do some x-rays, to make sure his bones were still intact and were not fractured," the doctor said while Shawn laid still with an IV coming out of his left arm and he would close his eyes periodically.

After two hours, he was x-rayed and placed in the ICU, as his condition was deemed 'critical.'

He was assigned two nurses, who were in charge of evaluating him and checking his vitals. He was hooked up with wires to monitor his heart and vitals. But they still wanted to check directly.

"How are you feeling, Shawn?" One of the nurses asked while checking his breathing, which was a little raspy, but he was doing ok.

"Just tired," he muttered.

"Are you thirsty?" The nurse asked while finishing up, and he nodded with his sunken and pale eyes.

"Ok. I'll get you some water and Gatorade, ok?" She asked; Shawn nodded as he laid on his back with pillows under his head.

The doctor who was in charge was Dr. Johnson. He came in after every fifteen minutes as he was concern about Shawn, as he had a seven-year-old son, who was in the ICU for three years with Pneumonia and almost died, but he pulled through.

"Are my parents coming in?" He asked with a muttered tone.

Dr. Johnson looked at him with concerned eyes and said, "Yes, Shawn. They're on their way, but first things first, we have to make sure you're going to pull through. Your x-rays looked good, but we did draw some blood," he said as Shawn didn't know they did that.

"When did you do that?" He asked while the nurse came in with his ice water and a small Gatorade bottle.

"We did it while you were coming and going. We were able to do this through your IV. Now, please drink your water and Gatorade slowly," Dr. Johnson suggested with concern as the nurse used the bed pedal and lifted Shawn as he was almost sitting up, and she slowly gave him water.

He took some sips, and then she switched to the Gatorade. "This will help your body rehydrate and get some potassium back. You lost a lot of nutrients in that shack," Dr. Johnson said as the nurse guided Shawn in his weakened and kept switching drinks for him.

"Nice and slow, Shawn," she said while seeing that Shawn was significantly thirty as his lips were dried and cracked.

"Thank you," Shawn muttered to Dr. Johnson and he smiled and gently padded Shawn on the foot and left the room.

"Is there a way I can get some food?" He asked with a muttered tone.

"I think we can arrange something," the nurse said, and Shawn gently smiled a little as she kept helping with his fluid intake.

Chapter Twenty-Eight

Shawn's family arrived with anticipation of seeing his ailing son.

They arrived at the hospital with an eagerness to see Shawn.

They walked through the ER's entrance as the double doors opened, and all four were inside and went to the front desk.

"How may I help you?" The receptionist asked while seeing the family a little 'excited.'

"Yes, we were told they found our son, Shawn Patterson. He was taken to his hospital," Terri said while Ted were holding hands with his daughters, eager to see their brother.

The receptionist asked for a date of birth, and she was checking the ER log and then, "Oh yes, please wait in the waiting room while a nurse comes and gets you."

"Why do we have to wait!? We were told he was here..." Terri said with an irritated tone.

"You should let them in," A voice from behind them spoke, and it was Det. Mitchell.

"Who are you, sir?" The receptionist asked with a confused look.

"I'm Detective Paul Mitchell, and I am the detective who helped with their case," Det. Mitchell said with a slight smile while the family watched on. Det. Mitchell approached the desk, and two security guards approached him.

He smiled at the guards and showed his badge. They looked at it with a stern look and nodded.

"He's not quiet ready to be seen yet, but I'll let you know," the receptionist said with a firm tone and Det. Mitchell nodded and thanked her. He guided the family to the waiting room, which had seven visitors.

They found chairs and sat down. Terri glanced at Det. Mitchell asked, "Why are you here? I thought there was no hope of finding Shawn. You had given up. Why?" She asked with a firm tone as some visitors looked on with curious eyes.

"I understand that you're little upset, Mrs. Patterson, but you have to understand, I'm dealing with a killer right now, also. I only had one other person helping me with both cases. You do realize that are some people in this state, that are still missing?" Det. Mitchell asked while trying to make Terri understand.

"I'm just basing everything you told us, that's all. Do *you* understand what it's like to have a missing child...*someone* took him, and with the graces of God...we got him!" Her firm tone started to make Ted and Det. Mitchell slightly uncomfortable, but Ted was on his wife's side, but he still felt guilty as it happened while he was sleeping at the time.

Paul looked down at the tile floor, trying to be calm and not raise his tone as he felt he was being blamed for Shawn's disappearance, but he didn't understand their family's significant sadness.

"I don't understand whatsoever! Yes, I have a teenage daughter and I can only imagine what you went through, but it wasn't my fault nor anyone on the force...we *did* the best we could do...Mrs. Patterson," Paul said and Terri looked at him and she got up and went for a walk. The girls got up and joined her.

Ted and Paul sat a chair apart from each other and briefly looked at each other.

"How are you dealing with all of this, Mr. Patterson?"

"I'm___doing better now that Shawn was found," Ted said with a relieved tone.

"I'm sorry if Terri was abrupt with you...she's been under a lot of stress," Ted said while sitting back in the plastic chair with the thin padding.

"No worries, Sir. I'm just glad we found your son. One positive thing is going on right now," Det. Mitchell said as Ted looked on and could see that the detective was struggling a little with the case.

"How's the whole 'Rest Area Killer' thing going? I heard from the news that one of the survivors called him, 'Duke?': Ted asked while seeing Det. Mitchell was not surprised.

"Yeah, it's kinda true. He's called 'Duke.' We don't know why, but I don't know if he was a fan of John Wayne or something," Det. Mitchell sat back in his chair while looking at Ted.

"That's crazy to hear," Ted said while starting to explain what he said.

"It sure is," Paul smiled a little.

"My Dad's name was Duke. He died when I was young and was good to me, but he was not the most affectionate dad, but he was ok to me," Ted said while showing some sadness in his tone as Det. Mitchell looked on.

"I'm sorry about your loss. How did he die?"

"Honestly, it was a weird day for me. He died by gunfire, but my mother brought in a child psychiatrist, and supposedly, they made me forget," Ted chuckled a little, and Det. Mitchell smiled.

"So, she got a shrink, and he did a 'mind trick,' trying to have me forget, but it didn't work too well as I remembered some stuff."

"I'm sorry about your dad. What about your mother?" Det. Mitchell asked while a visitor was called into the backroom.

"She died years ago when I just got married. She died of a heart attack. According to the doctors, she died in her sleep."

"Man, I'm sorry about your losses. At least, now...you have something to looked forward to," Det. Mitchell pointed to the backroom, where their son, Shawn was being seen.

"Yeah, I'm so relieved that that older couple found him in that horrible shack," Ted said with relief in his tone.

"Do you know who took him that day?" Ted asked with a curious tone.

"Honestly, we have no suspects, but *this* person who took him and kept him alive must have some reason...I would think?" Det. Mitchell was unsure as he was honest with Ted.

"Do you think this 'Duke' guy had anything to do with it?" Ted asked with a curious look.

Det. Mitchell got up and stretched his back. "Honestly, I don't know. Why would he kidnap your son and kill others?" Det. Mitchell asked, not knowing the proper answer.

Ted shrugged his shoulders as Terri came back with the girls.

"Ok. You can go in now," A nurse said as she stood by the double doors and waited for the Patterson family. As they smiled with relief, Ted got up and walked with his family while Det. Mitchell left as he would need to, at some point, interview Shawn and ask some questions, but tonight was not that night. He thought and walked out of the hospital and left. He went home while Ted, Terri, and the girls reunited with Shawn.

Chapter Twenty-Nine

Tears flowed as the Patterson family was together again. Terri hugged Shawn's frail frame. Shawn smiled as there was a nurse who had just finished up making he had dranked the majority of his water and Gatorade.

"How are you doing, baby?" Terri asked while holding his hand, feeling his hand cold and rigid.

"I'm ok, Mom." He muttered.

"Hey, son...how are you feeling?" Ted asked with watery eyes.

The girls came up and gave Shawn gentle hugs. They had watery eyes as the family gathered around while the nurse left, leaving the family alone as she could feel and see their joy.

"I'm___alright, Daddy..." Shawn said while trembling.

"What's wrong?" Terri asked with a firm tone.

"It's...hard for me...'cause the person..who...took...was a guy," Shawn said while his voice trembled. Ted felt guilty as he knew that Shawn was not talking about him, but *Shawn said that a male had taken him...that SON OF BITCH!* Ted thought with an angered tone.

"I'm sorry, Shawn." Ted said while backing off a little as Terri looked on and asked, "Why did you call him, Daddy?" Terri asked with a firm tone. She didn't quite understand why he would call his father that.

"It's not Dad, Mom...the guy that took me...sounded a little like him, but his tone was deeper and more like crooked," Shawn spoke a little better as Terri looked at Ted with a firm look.

*Shawn had called Ted that when he was a little younger or in trouble...*Terri thought.

Ted looked on with a surprised look.

"What crooked voice, Shawn?" Terri asked.

"You know when you do a voice that is a little deeper and has a slight accent?"

"Yes, like someone acting as a cowboy? Or someone with an accent from the South?" Terri asked with a curious tone.

"That's it! The southern accent. Also, he was a little taller but wearing cowboy boots..." Shawn was talking with a low and fluent tone.

"Dad, I'm sorry for scaring you...I know you were sleeping, but this guy came up from behind and..." Shawn started to develop tears, and Terri embraced him. Ted was amazed by his son's statement. Fuck me! What he just described...was the fuckin' 'Rest Area Killer...' Shit! Ted thought as Shawn looked at him and called him over. Ted embraced his son as tears flowed heavily, and Terri placed her hand on Ted's shoulders, and the girls watched on while another nurse started her shift and she would take vitals.

Chapter Thirty

Det. Mitchell got home as he drove his car into the driveway and was dead tired. He got out of his car and walked into his home. His daughter was already asleep as he stopped, gently opened her bedroom door, and could see her sleeping peacefully.

Paul walked into the kitchen, placed his badge on the kitchen table, walked over to the fridge, and took out a cold Coors Lite beer.

He walked around the kitchen while drinking his beer and was hungry. *I should have grabbed something for dinner, but I wasn't in the mood for it...*He thought while walking over to the cupboard that had snacks and cans of food. He decided to eat beefaroni for dinner.

He opened the can and poured it into a bowl on the counter.

He knew it was clean because he took it out of the dishwasher the other day but forgot to put it away. He placed the bowl into the microwave with a paper towel covering it as it would splatter all over the microwave.

He put it on for two minutes and fifty seconds. While waiting, he picked up his beer, took a sip, walked into the living room, and decided to turn on the TV.

The smell of the beefaroni filled the house as he walked around and enjoyed his cold one. *Well, I might have to grab another cold one while I eat.* He thought the news came on while his food was cooking and talked about the Patterson family arriving at Maine General Hospital.

"Oh shit! They're gonna harp on that family!" He said out loud while drinking the last drop of his beer. He walked into the kitchen, disgusted that the media found out, the microwave went off, and his food was ready.

Paul took out his food, and while almost burning his fingertips, he gripped it with a bit, bringing it into the living room while walking back to the kitchen and grabbing another cold beer. He also grabbed a fork from a drawer with disorganized utensils.

He brought a paper towel with him also and sat on the couch where his delicious microwave food sat, with steam sloping upwards out of the bowl. He placed the bowl with a paper towel on his lap and gently indulged himself while taking sips of his beer to cool the food in his mouth.

He watched on as the news was outside the hospital in a live report, and Paul shook his head with disbelief and disgust. *Why can't these fuckin' reporters leave this family alone...I mean, come on! They just got together with their son!* Paul ate more of his food as he took a sip of his beer and watched on.

Chapter Thirty-One

Hours passed, and it was two in the morning. Paulie Mills was self-employed and had her website as she made fabrics and sold perfume. She was financially set and had no family attachments.

She was fifty-eight and had been married once. She was married to an abuser; who was controlling, and one night, Paulie had enough after her husband took it upon himself and smacked her in the face, all because she didn't get Chinese takeout for him.

She was heading to Newport, where she lived, and was coming from Portland, where she attended a fabric show and made some sales. *I'm glad some people who bought my perfume and fabrics were interested in spending cold cash today.* She smiled as she had to stop due to the champagne she dranked, and felt the urge go to the bathroom.

With her short-feathered, grayish hair and black-rimmed glasses, she was trying to go to Newport without stopping, but she knew that was not happening. *I knew I should of use the restroom before leaving...now, I gotta piss!* She thought while seeing a sign that said, **Rest Area Two Miles.**

"Well, shit...over two in the morning and I have to stop at the one place where all of those killings been happening," Paulie said outloud as she was now one mile from the now, infamous rest area.

She thought about pulling the car to the side of the highway and relieving herself with the urge getting worse. *I could just park my car, but who knows if some weirdo or a state trooper pulls over and sees my fat ass hanging in the wind...that would be a sight for anyone to see...*She jokingly thought while her car was drawing closer to the rest area.

She was slightly nervous as she was a little concerned about who might be there. *Alright, here we go...*She pulled her car into the rest area and saw three other vehicles.

Well, I see two cars in the back and a truck up front...someone is either getting laid or just getting off. FUCK! My husband got off quickly, sometimes in his pants or on the way to my pleasure spot. I'm glad the fucker died of a cardiac arrest, and his insurance money helped spawn my business. She thought while getting out of her car and then proceeded to the trunk of her car and decided to take a tire wrench with her.

She took it out as it was a little rusty, but she knew it could do a job on some *weirdo who tried to make a move on me.* She thought while carrying the tire wrench and slowly walking up to the rest area as the lights shined in specific areas such as the entrances and back of the rest area. There was minimal lighting in the parking area.

She slowly walked into the women's restroom with the tire wrench gripped tightly in her right hand as she walked in and looked around, a little disgusted by the graffiti and the smell of the rest area. *Man, this is one shithole!* She looked into each stall, where there were six stalls.

She opened the stall door, as there were dried pieces of gum, tissues, and other unrecognizable stuff as Paulie held herself, trying not to urinate in her pants as she was on the verge of letting go.

Got to get this goin', or I'm going to piss my pants! She thought while reaching down to the toilet paper, unreeling it, placing it on the toilet seat, and using it as a toilet seat cover.

She placed the tire wrench on the side as it was just under the toilet paper dispenser and she pulled down her pants and started to relieve herself. *Holy shit! That feels friggin' good!* She said with a slight smile as she sat and waited, just in case it was one of those deals where you went, but had to go again a minute later.

Here we go...more pissing! Paulie sat on the toilet with her pants down and peeing as she remembered she had her cell and decided to take it out of her back pocket and check her social media.

Five minutes passed, and she could not believe how much wine was going through her. *Well, it serves me right to drink wine and nothing else. It would be best to get everything else and not worry about ten minutes on the pike.* She thought while logging into her social media while a little irritated.

The restroom door opened, and Paulie heard footsteps. They were solid like thick shoes. Paulie looked at her stall and was relieved it was locked. The person that walked in, was two stalls from her and Paulie heard the person flushing the toilet and making disgruntle sounds as the person 'grossed' out by what they were seeing.

Paulie smiled as she took some pleasure as she heard the person cleaning the toilet they were going to be using, and Paulie remained silent as she hoped no one knew she was in there. *I hate places like these!* She nervously thought while relieving herself; the person in the other stall heard her go to the bathroom. It was a little paranoia on Paulie's part.

Come on, bladder...stop PISSIN'! Paulie thought with a frustrated look, and she was listening to the person sitting on their dirty and disgusting nighttime throne. The other person flushed the toilet, and Paulie heard them finishing up and wiping themselves as the echoes filled the restroom.

Paulie took some toilet paper and got up while wiping herself. Suddenly, the urge kept coming, and she peed more. *I am so fuckin' done with wine! This is bullshit!* Paulie thought with frustration.

Suddenly, the restroom door opened and closed as the other person had left and another person had come in. The footsteps were heavier, and they were drawing nearer where Paulie was.

A nervous look grew on her face as she listened to the heavier footsteps, and she could hear getting closer; the stall door next to her opened, and a person walked in it. Paulie could hear the footing was heavier, and she was curious about what kind of shoes the woman was wearing.

Paulie could see the heels as the person next to her was not wearing heels or shoes but cowboy boots. Paulie remained calm as she knew women do wear cowboy boots. She hoped her bladder was done. *I wanna get the fuck out of here!* She thought while attempting to get up, and then, she was done! She decided to get off as it seemed her bladder was finally calm.

She wiped herself and quickly pulled up her pants. She flushed the toilet, picked up her phone, and exited the stall. She started washing her hands while her cell was in her back pocket, but suddenly, she forgot to grab the tire wrench. *Shit! I need that!* She nervously thought as she quickly returned to the stall and picked it up; suddenly, she heard a slight laugh, a man's tone.

Out of desperation, she gripped the tire wrench tightly and locked the stall door. She stood, holding the tire wrench tightly in her grasp and the other stall door opened and the heavy footsteps were heard as she was able to see them leading to the sink.

She could hear the person washing their hands and then, exiting while having a slight laugh. *WHAT THE FUCK WAS THAT ALL ABOUT!?* She thought while deciding to wait a minute before exiting.

She slowly opened the door while looking both ways, making sure there was no one on either side and then she made her way to the exit while holding the tire wrench. She rushed out of the exit and to her car. She reached out for the car's door and didn't know if she had locked it, but it was unlocked.

She got into the car while placing the tire wrench in the passenger side, and then, she heard the laugh and BOOM! She was hit in the head, and she fought back. Her eyes were glazy, and the pain was excruciating. She had no idea what had happened, but then she looked over and saw a man exiting the back door of her car and then. He walked around and opened the passenger door.

She picked up the tire wrench and took a swing, but he stopped her, pulled it away from her, and then said, "Time to die, bitch!" He said, and swung the tire wrench numerous times, bashing her sockets, cheeks, bones, and head. The man left the scene, and hours later, Paulie was found dead with an eyeball that fell to the floor of her car while the other dangled from her eye socket.

Chapter Thirty-Two

Shawn woke up in the morning. He had slept off and on during the night. The hospital had given him pain meds as he complained of his head hurting slightly. This was due to dehydration. Even though he had been given liquids from his IV and dranked a lot, he still had a long way to go.

Terri was asleep in the chair that was next to Shawn. He looked over with his pale face and he looked around for his father and his sisters, but they were no where in sight.

Shawn reached with his arm and picked up the half-full of water as the ice had melted, but Shawn didn't care. He took a drink and placed it back on the patient's table.

The TV was playing as cartoons were on, and Shawn looked on while looking sporadically at his mother. The nurse brought a breakfast menu for Shawn to look at.

"Hi, Shawn; how are you feeling?" She asked while she placed the small menu onto the table, and then, she walked to his other side and started taking vitals.

"I'm ok. My throat is a little dry," he said while he laid back, and the nurse checked his vitals.

"Well, it's gonna take a while. Your body needs liquids, but I think you might go home by tomorrow or in a couple of days, she said while checking his blood pressure and looking at the TV.

"Can I eat anything?" Shawn looked up at the nurse with his innocent and sunken eyes and she replied, "Absolutely!" She said while while smiling. She finished taking his vitals.

"Ok. What do you want for breakfast?" She asked while looking at him and seeing him shake a little as he was not at full strength.

He looked at the menu. "Can I have cereal, like *Fruit Loops* with orange juice and some toast, please?" He asked with a polite tone.

""It will be done!"

"Can Mom have some too?" He asked, his voice still a little raspy, but she understood his question.

"Yeah, when she wakes up, she can get some too. I'll keep the menu on the table, okay?"

"Ok." He responded while watching cartoons.

The nurse left and went to get Shawn more water and another IV bag. His current one was running low.

Terri stirred, as she was waking and her vision was little a foggy, but then, she was waking up.

"Hey, hun. How are you feeling?" She asked while getting up and kissing his forehead.

"I'm ok. I'm getting breakfast. The nurse said you get some too, if you want," he said while pointing to the menu and Terri smiled and responded. "Sounds good to me."

"Do you know where Dad is?" Shawn turned his head, asking his mother while Terri was looking at the menu.

"He brought your sisters home and I think that they were getting some sleep," she said while checking her cell and not seeing any messages.

"What day is it?" He asked while Terri checked her messages and responded, "It's Wednesday. They also might be at school, but that's a long night. Everyone at the house must be sleeping," Terri smiled, and Shawn nodded.

"The nurse said I might be going home by tomorrow or in a couple of days, depending on what the doctor says."

"Yeah, that's probably you're getting better, but we'll see what the doctor says. Did the nurse say when he would be coming in?"

"No. She just said he would be coming in sometime today," he explained while watching cartoons.

Terri glanced at Shawn and smiled. She was so relieved that she was sitting in the hospital with her son than at a funeral home.

Terri got up and kissed her son on the forehead once again before texting Ted on her cell.

Chapter Thirty-Three

Another familiar site for Det. Mitchell as he stood by the car of another victim at the Augusta Rest Area. *Here we go again....and again!* He thought while seeing blood on the interior side of the driver's side door.

Capt. Morse was on sight as Det. Mitchell was waiting for his new partner, whom he had promoted. "So, I heard you got a new partner without consulting me first?" The expression on Capt. Morse's face was not amusing.

"Yeah, where is he?" Det. Mitchell was waiting for him.

"He's not coming, Paul! His superiors decided they needed him and I didn't authorize it either," she said while seeing Paul growing frustrated.

"YOU GOT TO BE KIDDIN'!" He said outloud.

"Easy, detective. I'm with you and we also are expecting an informant tomorrow at 10:AM. I expect you to be there," she said firmly while briefly looking at the car.

Det. Mitchell grew frustrated. "How am I supposed to solve this *damn* case without any frickin' help!"

"Like I said, I'm with you and this informant will be also."

"What's the person's name?" Det. Mitchell asked while the CSI heard the two disagree.

"FBI Agent Informant Benton."

"So, FBI Agent Informant Benton is coming tomorrow. Am I supposed to take his orders?" Det. Mitchell did a sarcastic look and Capt. Morse said, "It's unnecessary, but I will tell you, he's been around!" She explained and started to focus on the homicide at hand.

"So, what happened here?" Capt. Morse asked a frustrated Det. Mitchell, but he started to focus on the matter also.

He took out his handy pen. He used it for pointing to particular items on a scene.

"He changed his strategy a little," Det. Mitchell said while starting to explain to Capt. Morse.

"If you look over here, he was in the back of the car and then, he came around and killed her," he was explaining.

"How do you know that?" Capt. Morse asked with a questionable look.

"The backseat has a slight imprint, as if someone had been laying, waiting for the victim to arrive. We also might have found an imprint of a boot as there was water, that seemed to spill and the killer had stepped in it," Det. Mitchell was explaining as Capt. Morse was growing a little excited.

"I want to make sure we check every bit of this car. Who was the victim?" She asked while the victim was still in the car, blood covered her as well as the front seats, the staring wheel and the dashboard.

"Will do, but this is *something* with this one," Det. Mitchell started to explain his opinion.

"What do you mean?" Capt. Morse asked while they were both kneeling as CSI watched on.

"Why did he bash her face in like that?" Det. Mitchell asked while pointing to the tire wrench that was used.

"You don't think this is the same person, do you?" She asked with a curious look as Det. Mitchell pickup the tire wrench, which was already in a sealed zip lock bag and he turned to her.

"I'm not sure, but this is not his style."

"What happened here was someone filled with hatred and fury towards the victim. I'm unsure if this is the same killer," Det. Mitchell explained as they stood up, and Capt. Morse was in disbelief.

"If we have another killer, we're in deep trouble," Capt. Morse said with a frustrated tone.

"I know, but we need a print on this weapon and trace that footprint we found in the backseat. This person was a little sloppy in comparison to the other murders."

Capt. Morse looked at Det. Mitchell and told, "We need to be quiet on this, because I don't need the commissioner nor the Governor on my case," she said with a firm and concern tone.

"Captain, I get it, but you took my help away, and then, you have some kind investigator coming tomorrow and make us look like idiots!" He said firmly, and Capt. Morse stared at him and walked off.

"We found something else," one of the CSI agents said while grabbing a sealed ziplock bag and showing Det. Mitchell.

"What we found was; a piece of hair not matching the victim's and could be the attacker," he explained as Det. Mitchell smiled and asked to have it analyzed.

"That's awesome! We need to find out anything we can with this hair, the footprint, and possible prints on the murder weapon."

"Will do."

Det. Mitchell saw Capt. Morse got into her car and drove off. Det. Mitchell walked away, spotted two news vans coming in, and decided to leave. *I won't be around for this shitstorm to happen!* While pacing quickly to his car, he thought, but one of the reporters blocked him, and Det. Mitchell was forced to do an interview.

"What we found was another victim. This happened sometime overnight."

"Are these murders related to the Rest Area Killer?" One of the reporters asked while Det. Mitchell had almost to close his eyes as the camera lights were almost too bright. **"As of right now, we don't know, nor can we assume they are."**

"What is the victim's name?"

"I can't reveal anything yet, because we don't know, and we'll keep you informed."

"Detective Mitchell, what's the status of the child who was found? Is he able to do an interview?"

"You will have to wait and see, but also, his parents have a say in that. Thank you."

Det. Mitchell walked through the rest of the reporters, got into his car, and drove off. He was heading back to the station, hoping that something had been found about the killer.

Chapter Thirty-Four

Lauri woke up while getting ready for school. Even though they were at the hospital late last night, she decided to get ready and go to school. Her mind was filled with joy and alarming thoughts. *The guy who took my little bro, where is he?* She thought while combing her hair and looking into the bathroom mirror.

Afterward, she went downstairs, and her sister was already ready and eating cereal. She looked around for her father, who was sleeping on the couch with an ice pack near his head. Lauri picked it up and placed it in the freezer. *Dad must have one of those headaches again.* Lauri thought while pulling up the fleece blanket to his neck and gently tucking it in.

When doing so, her fingertips touched his neck, which was cold. She checked his forehead with the palm of her hand. Her mother taught her to do this when someone might be sick and running a fever. *Wow! Dad, you are cold!...* Lauri thought with a concerned look, and she ensured he was warm enough.

Afterward, she walked back into the kitchen, took a strawberry pop tart, and placed it into the toaster.

"You're ready before me!" Lauri smiled as Marla was dressed and finishing up her cereal.

"I thought we were going to see Shawn?" Marla asked before another spoonful of cereal entered her mouth, and milk dripped from her lips.

"We'll probably go see him after school or something," Lauri assumed that was the case. She also knew her father was losing his job, and he was upset about the matter. *I know Dad is losing his job to some takeover or something.* She thought while her pop tart popped up, and Lauri placed it on a paper towel sheet and started indulging herself.

"Do you think Shawn will be ok?" Marla asked while Lauri sat next to her at the kitchen table. Lauri looked up at her and said, "Shawn will be ok. He's at the hospital and will be fine."

"Do you think they will get the guy who took him?" Marla asked with an innocent tone before eating more of her cereal.

It was a question that Lauri didn't want to answer as she was too bothered by someone taking their brother. *I can imagine they'll get the guy who took our brother. I'm glad he's ok.* She thought while trying not to cry and glanced over at her sister, whose eyes were watery. Lauri got up, walked over to Marla, and embraced her.

They were both crying as Lauri kissed Marla's forehead and asked her to prepare for school.

"Alright, now I'm gonna have to touch up on my makeup," Lauri said with a slight chuckle, and she smiled and offered to help.

"Can I help you?" Marla asked while Lauri looked at her and nodded.

"Sure. We need to brush our teeth afterward, agreed?" Lauri put out her pinky finger, and Marla linked up with hers, both pinky swore.

Chapter Thirty-Five

Ted slowly got up while feeling heavy like weights. The headache he had last night was terrible. He remembered when coming home, and the girls went to bed while he had an ice pack and crashed on the sofa. *Man, that was some crazy fuckin' headache last night!* He thought while deciding to make some coffee. He looked at the time, and it was ten thirty. He was supposed to be at work right now, but *fuck it! I'm getting let go, so why should I give a shit!* The coffee was brewing while he walked to the living room's end table and checked his text messages.

There were two from Terri and a couple from work, and that was it. The coffee was made, and he put non-dairy creamer in it, stirred it, and then went back into the living room and sat down.

He was going through the channels while the steam from his coffee arose into the air with a soothing, defined aroma. He immediately took a sip as the coffee was what he needed. With his job, he didn't care about going as much as watching TV and drinking his coffee. *Terri told her work late last night about the news, and her boss told her to take a few days off if necessary. She's lucky they like her. My new job tells me to go fuck myself!* Ted thought with an angered tone.

He texted his boss and told him that they found Shawn, and he was at the hospital last night and wouldn't be in for a couple of days. Of course, as Ted suspected, he never got a response.

While the TV was on and Ted was drinking his coffee, he decided to go online with his cell and look up job opportunities in Maine. He did have accounts with ZipRecruiter and Indeed.

"Well, there's a bunch of jobs, but none that I'm looking at," he said to himself while he had some interest, but he did like his job and hoped it would work out, but it's not going to happen. He took another drink of his coffee and would get ready and be ready and wait for the girls to come home from school and see Shawn.

The text message he received from Terri was that they were moving him to a room, and he could be in the hospital for a couple more days.

Ted understood the hospital's concerns. He texted Terri and told her his plan, and she gave him the thumbs-up meme.

***

"Suspects are always one step ahead of the police, whether you like it or not, but that's how serial killers work! They sometimes don't know what or why they do what they're doing, but in the end, for some, it's about control, and for others, it's about power," FBI Agent Benton said while standing in the conference room and talking to some state troopers from their districts. Det. Mitchell, along with Capt. Morse sat in the back and watched. Det. Mitchell was already annoyed as Capt. Morse looked at him with slight irritation.

Agent Benton stood tall with his 5'11 frame, combed hair, and thick-rimmed glasses. He pointed to pictures of victims from notorious murders such as 'Son Of Sam,' 'Ted Bundy,' and 'The Night Stalker.'

"These are killings for which the killer had some remorse, like, for example, you see this victim had her face covered up, the killer felt remorse." The picture was a little disturbing to some of the attendees.

"Hello, Det. Mitchell. Can you explain what's going on here with the killings?" Agent Benton asked while staring at Det. Mitchell with a firm look. Det. Mitchell didn't know what to say until Agent Benton spoke again.

"Pertaining to the killings in Maine such as 'The Rest Area Killer,' that case should have already resolved." His tone was offensive to some of the troopers, while Det. Mitchell looked at him with a firm look.

"How do you figure?" Det. Mitchell asked with a firm tone.

"Well, for starters, there's no task force! Second, I should have been brought in when this case was blown open. Third, I would have done a stakeout or had an undercover officer at the rest area," he explained, and Det. Mitchell rolled his eyes and smirked, and looked at Capt. Morse.

"I wanted some of those, but my authority was overruled, right Captain?" Det. Mitchell said while glancing at Capt. Morse, who gave him a look, that said, GO FUCK YOURSELF!

"We wanted to do those, but the commissioner said no," she explained while fuming and looking at Det. Mitchell.

Other officers and detectives looked on with enjoyment. "The commissioner makes the calls with everything in Maine?" Agent Benton asked with a confused look.

"Yes, that's correct."

"This is strictly a serial killer case, and do you know what needs to be done? Look at the 'Son Of Sam' and 'The Boston Strangler.' they had a task force. I might have to talk with the commissioner," he said firmly.

"I'll contact him," Capt. Morse responded while Det. Mitchell smirked and looked at Agent Benton and Capt. Morse. *There is a frickin' GOD! Everything I wanted to do, and I said no. Thank you, Mr. Benton...you fuckin' pencil pusher!* Det. Mitchell thought while smirking.

"With this case, everything needs to be reviewed and evaluated. One little thing that is missed could cost your suspect and this case," Agent Benton explained as the rest of the officials looked on.

Chapter Thirty-Six

Shawn was being moved to his room, which was 17A. It was on the other side of the hospital, and Terri would text Ted, letting him know where they were moving Shawn. Terri followed as the staff was moving him out of the ICU.

Terri had texted Ted where they were moving their son. She got a text back from him, indicating that the headaches were happening and that he would be there later with the girls. Terri understood as she followed the staff as they pushed his bed, passed rooms, and went through hallways.

Shawn glanced at the passing lights as he layed still on his moving bed while he could hear his mother behind him as they were almost at his room. The staff wheeled him into his room, and Shawn sat up a little as he scanned the room, which showed it had two occupants.

Terri walked into and did the same. She was curious if anyone would be his roommate. "Is there anyone else that will be in this room with him?" She asked with a curious tone.

The staff looked at her and said, "Not at the moment; they asked Shawn to sit up while they lifted him onto the bed and rolled the other bed out of the room. Within seconds, two nurses came in and started to check his vitals while the one checked his IV.

"This one can go for another of days, but it may have to be changed," the evaluating nurse said to the one checking Shawn's vitals. "Whatever works, I guess. We don't know if the doctor will discharge him yet." She said while Shawn looked on with the blanket gently covering his feet as Terri watched.

"Is the doctor planning to discharge him soon?" Terri asked with a curious look as she didn't know and assumed it would be for a while since Shawn was transferred.

"It's hard to tell. Shawn was transferred because he's improved, but we still want to keep an eye on him for now," the vital nurse said and smiled at Shawn. Terri nodded and appreciated the doctor's way of thinking. *That makes sense. I'm glad he's here and not some hospital that ignored their patients.* Terri thought while the vital's nurse asked if Shawn wanted something and asked for ginger ale.

"Okay. How about you?" She looked at Terri and said, "I'll have what he's having." She smiled and thanked her.

Terri walked over to Shawn and held his wrist gently. "How are you feeling, honey?"

"I'm okay, but still a little tired. Are Dad and the girls coming back?" He asked while his voice was still a little raspy.

"Yeah, Dad's having one of those headaches right now, but he'll push through it, and he's gonna wait for the girls to come home from school, and then, they'll be over."

"Did you tell Dad where I am?"

"Sure did, honey," Terri smiled, and Shawn smiled, and Terri decided to turn the TV on for him.

Chapter Thirty-Seven

Det. Mitchell was at the rest area. He'd pictured himself as the killer walking and waiting for the next victim. *This guy must use a vehicle unless he lives nearby, walks through the woods, and waits to see who drives up.* He thought.

Det. Mitchell took a walk; he first thought to put a State license plate in the window of his vehicle and said, **State Government Detective.** Just in case, a state trooper pulled in and saw a mysterious man walking around.

After doing so, he went around the back of the building and saw the path where people would meet up and have a 'pow wow.' He continued walking up the path where his investigators had gone, and there was still caution tape on the ground with some trash.

There were bushes on both sides of the path; as he approached the end, it was like a turnaround, but something in his eye caught his attention, and he put his hand by his firearm. He walked over, and it was another path, but this one was not part of the original layout of the rest area.

He walked_on it while fighting with branches and pricklier bushes ticking at him, and he walked further for another fifteen minutes, and he stopped only to realize that the rest area was no longer in sight. *What the hell is this? I can't even see them building, but I can hear the traffic on the highway; but what the hell is that?* He thought while pulling out pieces of brush from his clothes. He knew it was a path based on the outline, but it had been overgrown.

A house with shingles tangling off the roof and the paint was peeled as it stood about twenty yards from the path. It was hidden from the rest area, and he was surprised that he and his officers didn't see it. *The house is well hidden from the highway and unnoticeable to anyone who goes to the rest area.* Det. Mitchell thought while cautiously approaching the house.

He walked towards the house as there were rusted metal oil barrows around the house. Most were in the front of the house. Det. Mitchell looked around cautiously, knowing someone could be home, and then suddenly, as he came to the front, a Black Ford Ranger with an extended cabin was parked in front of the old house with a dirt driveway.

Det. Mitchell was in front of the house as he looked at the truck, got his little notepad out, and wrote down the license plates that read **DUKE1.**

Well, that's interesting. That's the same truck with the same license plate seen leaving that house in Durham. Det. Mitchell thought while a nervousness started to build within; he was cautious as he made his way to the front, and he decided to withdraw his firearm and was now scanning the area.

Det. Mitchell kept his eye on the front door while looking over the truck; something smelled like rotten eggs, and sure enough, he looked in the front seat. Blood was on the front seat as he looked through the passenger window. He was tempted to open the door but didn't want to mess with it as he was concerned about erasing any possible fingerprints.

He finally made his way to the front door, where the screen was partially ripped, the door was on two hinges, and the third was broken. He grasped his firearm tightly, waiting for the suspect to surprise him, but nothing.

He opened the door as it creaked, and Det. Mitchell rolled his eyes, knowing that there was a possibility he had just blown his cover, but as he slowly walked into the old house, the smell was very acrid. He held his nose and couldn't believe someone could live in these conditions. Cobwebs inherited the house and pieces of trash like empty food cans and burned newspapers.

The rugs were stained with blood also, with a wooden chair and a broken living room table that was cracked to the bottom.

Det. Mitchell continued to walk through the house, as his nerves were on a high and his heart was pounding.

Det. Mitchell couldn't believe someone lived here. *Fuckin' smell!* He thought while trying not to breathe too much.

Det. Mitchell continued his search throughout the house, first through the living room and then a bedroom where fleas and other bugs were spawning.

Maggots were engulfing themselves in an apple on the floor beside a bed. The apple had maybe five bites from someone who only wanted to snack a little, as Det. Mitchell continued his search throughout the house, and he saw something in the kitchen, and it was someone; he stayed low, held his firearm high, and then listened, hoping to hear the person talk, but the person was at the kitchen table and was silent.

Det. Mitchell looked faithfully into the kitchen, and as he got closer, he saw a person sitting down at the kitchen table, but he finally made his way into the kitchen holding his firearm tightly; the person he saw at the table…was dead!

Det. Mitchell was alert and looked at the body tied up with duct tape in a chair.

Probably decaying so quickly because of our hot summer. What is that on his chest? There was a mark on the person's chest, which looked like a female.

Deidre, *it said.* Det. Mitchell couldn't believe his eyes as he saw a woman from some class or a conference. *She was dressed casually, with a button with her name on it.* The woman's footwear was black sandals, not the ones you wear at the beach, but these were more casual.

Det. Mitchell went to take out his cell, but he accidentally left it in the car. *Paul, you stupid son of bitch! How could you forget your cell...Stupid!* He thought he had walked passed the body.

He saw their dirty dishes in the sink. Det. Mitchell couldn't believe what he saw and thought *someone lived or had lived here. Holy cow!*

The kitchen floor was tile, and mold patches had protruded, especially near the sink area. Ahead of him was another bedroom, and he saw clothes on the carpeted floor, and then he saw another body, a female, whose clothes had been stripped as it looked to Det. Mitchell had been sexually assaulted.

Det. Mitchell went to the bedroom to examine her with his eyes and saw that her nose was broken. *Unbelievable*. He thought, and then his senses returned to the reality that the killer might still be here, *but where?* He thought.

This could be the Rest Area Killer I've been looking for, but where's the killer? Det. Mitchell thought. He walked away from the bed where the body was, and he saw a bathroom, and he walked into it and saw shaving cream all over the tub and toilet.

He's been here! There was hair on the dirty tile floor, and Det. Mitchell was disgusted by all of what he had seen so far, and he looked into another bedroom, and the room had a child's clothes scattered all over the floor. It belonged to some child, and there were pieces of duct tape everywhere.

He got closer, and suddenly, he heard someone walking into the house with the creaking of the screen door.

Det. Mitchell gathered his thoughts, and he had to hide. He hid in the bedroom with his firearm up and knelt on the floor nearest to the bed, but then he looked over and saw a closet and decided to hide in it. He got up and walked to the closet while trying to be quiet. There were a couple of cardboard boxes and clothes.

The footsteps were heavy, and he could hear them from the kitchen sounding on the floor. We're close to the kitchen. Det. Mitchell held his firearm tightly, waiting patiently for the person to enter the bedroom, and then he would try to arrest the suspect or be forced to take out the suspect.

The sounds of grunts were heard from the kitchen, and Det. Mitchell knew he was dealing with a male suspect, but he was a killer, with *those bodies being pure evidence*. He thought while his forehead grew sweaty.

The footsteps were very heavy, and he heard the man grunting more, and then he heard, "What the fuck is this?" The man asked harshly, and his voice cracked with a Texan tone. Det. Mitchell had to think that maybe he had left something around the table or in the kitchen, but something was *wrong! Shit! Did I leave something in the kitchen?* Det. Mitchell nervously thought.

"Oh, I see we have a visitor, kids." The man spoke while cracking a smile. Det. Mitchell held his weapon tightly, knowing he might have been discovered, but then… "Fuckin' mouse!" A hard stomp came from the kitchen and Det. Mitchell felt relieved that it was not him but a mouse.

He gathered his thoughts while waiting for the man to enter the bedroom, and then he would attack him.

"Hey, bitch! The sound came somewhere nearby, and Det. Mitchell knew the man was close, but *how close?* He thought, but he knew he had to be ready for something, but the footsteps started up again, and they headed for the other room on the other side of the kitchen, and *I can't wait to get this shit over with. Where is he?*

The heavy boots were banging and clinging as they were heard from all over the house, and as this went on, Det. Mitchell sat in a crouching position in the closet while almost sitting on one of the cardboard boxes, and he waited for the man to enter the room, but nothing.

A few minutes later, the sounds stopped, and it seemed as if the man had disappeared, and Det. Mitchell didn't move. He wanted to move as his legs were tired, but he was afraid to because he felt he would give away his position.

Det. Mitchell held his firearm tightly and felt his forearm growing tired, and put down the firearm and…Smash! A sound was heard from the kitchen as if *something* onto the floor.

The footsteps came into the kitchen once again, and Det. Mitchell held his firearm, hoping the man would enter the bedroom.

"Hey, Baby. YOU HAIRY BITCH! Fuckin' cat! Always in the way." A sudden scream from the kitchen and a cracking sound, and then a medium thump as it sounded like someone took their fist and hammered a car with it like a hammer.

He killed the cat! What the fuck is that all about? Poor kitty. I can't believe he killed a fucking cat! Det. Mitchell thought in disbelief.

"What a fucker!" Det. Mitchell said quietly, and then the footsteps were moving, and the sounds seemed to get closer to the bedroom, and Det. Mitchell felt what he said; the man heard.

As the footsteps grew closer, Det. Mitchell felt he had to act, but he was ready after years of force and experience. The footsteps were near the bedroom where Det. Mitchell was hiding, and then he heard a peal of low laughter and Det. Mitchell slowly rose to see if the man was in the bedroom, then…

Chapter Thirty-Eight

Shawn was up and around, gazing through the hospital room window as he wanted to go home. The dark memories of living in that old shack were like shadows; they only appeared partly when the light was shining.

He was disturbed by this whole matter and felt pressure to tell people like his parents, the police, and the hospital staff of his ordeal, but he wanted to forget. He wanted to forget being grabbed from behind and dragged like a bag of potatoes. He wanted to forget the cold and warm nights. The times he was eating stale bread and dranked smelly water. At times, the water tasted like pennies.

Terri came into the room, she walked up to her son, seeing how lost he seemed to be, and she put her arms around him, and he felt comfort knowing his Mom was there with him and that she was protecting him now.

"How are you feeling, honey?" She asked gently as she rubbed his back and then went around him, she wanted to see his face, and she saw his face, which was filled with loss and sadness.

"Shawn, are you all right?" She asked.

"Mom...I wanna go home," He said with a frustrated tone.

"That's ok. The doctor said he would be coming back. They want to make sure you're feeling a lot better, that's all," she said with reassurance. A worry grew on her face as she stared at Shawn, who lived with those nightmares that would haunt him day and night.

"What happened to you, Shawn?" She finally asked him, knowing he was feeling a little better.

"Mom, I don't want to remember?" He said while turning to her. Terri reached up and gently wiped his tears.

"Honey, I'm sorry for what happened to you. I'm sorry that Dad and I couldn't protect you...It's *our* fault for not protecting you," Terri cried, and Shawn embraced her.

"Mom, I don't blame you and Dad. The man who took me was very mean and..."

Shawn was unable to finish his sentence. Terri looked up at him, her eyes watery and her face flushed.

"Shawn, did *he*...do something to you that was not ok...like touch you..?" The words were spoken with hesitation as she feared he was.

Shawn was silent at first, and then he answered. "No, he *never* did."

Terri embraced him, and they both cried.

Terri pulled back a little and looked at him, and he did the same.

"Do you know what he looks like?" She asked.

"He said bad things to me and told me if I tried to escape, he would kill my family and me."

"Did you see his face, Shawn?" She asked while feeling anger building within her.

Shawn looked to the window, watching the leaves blow by the window as the cold November air blossomed.

"I did. He was wearing a mask." Shawn said and then turned to Terri.

"What did it look like?"

Shawn briefly closed his eyes, and then he told her. "It was a half mask, where the top of his face was covered, but the bottom part wasn't." He explained.

"Were there any details or writings on it?" Terri asked with a curious tone.

"It was like a skull part, but then, it wasn't. It's just scary," he said, looking out the window again.

"Honey, there's a detective that's going to want to ask those types of questions. Are you ready to answer them for him?"

At first, Shawn stared out the window, and then, he nodded.

Terri gently pulled away and walked out of the room, and Det. Mitchell walked in with Terri following.

"Hi Shawn, I'm Det. Mitchell, I'm the detective on your case. How are you feeling, son?" Paul asked with gentleness, and Shawn turned around and looked at him.

"I'm feeling better. Have you caught the man who took me?" Shawn asked with a straightforward question, which caught Det. Mitchell was off guard.

Det. Mitchell pulled up one of the chairs in the room and sat down, looking at Shawn while Terri stood by her son.

"To tell you the truth, I *think* I was at his house."

"You *were?*" Shawn and Terri were both stunned.

"I found an old home way in the back of the rest area and some old stuff, and then, I found this...is *this* yours?" Det. Mitchell pulled out a picture with Shawn and his family two years ago from Six Flags New England.

Det. Mitchell handed the photo to Shawn, and he and Terri glanced at the photo and were shocked by the find.

"Where exactly did you find this?" Terri asked with a firm tone.

"It was found on the living room table after the person in the house; left, and I saw it before rushing out. I also found a couple of bodies and other things," Det. Mitchell looked a little nervous as he didn't want to frighten Shawn.

"Oh, my God! Why would he have a photo of us!?" Terri asked with a firm tone as she glanced at the silent Shawn.

Shawn had no idea where this photo came from, and then he looked up at Det; Mitchell and asked, "Did you find a backpack?"

"We did, but it was empty. Why?"

"What is it, green with some stickers on it?" Shawn asked.

Det. Mitchell had to think, "Oh my God, we did! Did you bring that with you when you were in the restroom while your father was in the car?" Det. Mitchell asked while taking out his notepad and writing down Shawn's statement.

"When I was in the restroom, I ran back out, and Dad was sleeping, and I wanted to bring it with me."

"What was in it?" Det, Mitchell asked while briefly looking at Terri and then glancing back at Shawn.

"I had some comic books and a notepad. I like to draw and other things," Shawn explained, and Det. Mitchell jotted it down in his notepad.

"There were no comic books, but we did find your backpack. We're having prints running, seeing if we could get something."

Terri stood with Shawn, who needed to lie down, and Terri helped him while Det. Mitchell moved his chair out of the way.

Shawn got back into his bed and took a sip of his water.

"Is there anything you can tell me about what happened? Shawn?" Det. Mitchell looked at Shawn, showing concern; Shawn nodded and told Det. Mitchell everything.

Chapter Thirty-Nine

Ted was en route to the hospital to see Shawn. The girls were with them and anxious to see their brother. *I hope he's feeling better.* Lauri thought while she sat in the passenger seat, and Marla sat in the back.

"Dad, do you think Shawn will recover?" Lauri asked with a concerned tone.

Ted was initially reluctant to answer, afraid he might, but then he answered. "I think it's going to be a long process, but Shawn will be *almost* that he was, but those memories of what happened to him will never go away," Ted explained as his daughters looked at him and could hear his voice crackle a little. Tears rolled down his cheeks.

"Daddy? When will Shawn be coming home?" Marla asked innocently while looking through her window as they headed south to Augusta.

Ted wiped his tears away with his jacket sleeve and answered the question.

"Well, that depends on the doctor. Shawn will go home if he feels that Shawn is feeling better. I'm hoping it will be soon."

"Me too!" Marla said, and Lauri nodded.

"We're almost at the exit," Ted said while pointing his hand, and then, they made the turn.

"So, he's no longer in the ICU?" Lauri asked.

"Correct. He's in a room now, and Mom is with him," Ted explained as they went around the roundabouts.

"I gotta say, these roundabouts with the two lanes don't make any sense to me," Ted smirked, and his daughters smiled and were silent.

They took a right turn and were at Maine General Hospital. Excitement built within all three of them as Ted parked the vehicle, and they got out.

"What room is he in?" Lauri asked while they were walking towards the emergency room entrance.

"He's in 17A, according to Mom's text," Ted told her after checking his cell, and they entered the emergency room, unsure of what entrance they were supposed to take, and the receptionist helped them.

"Hello, we're looking for room 17A," Ted said.

"You want to go to that entrance, and they should be able to help you," the receptionist said, and Ted thanked her.

They walked out and decided to walk outside while the youngest and oldest were holding hands as Ted was anxious about seeing his son.

"Well, here we go!" He said they approached the receptionist, who was on his cell and had not acknowledged them while they walked through the main entrance.

"Hello, we're looking for 17A?" Ted asked, and the receptionist got off his cell and said, "Hello, yes. Are you family or friends?" He asked while looking at Ted and his daughters with a firm look.

"I'm the Dad, and these ladies are his sisters. His mother, Terri, should already be in the room with him," Ted explained, feeling anxious and a little irritated.

The receptionist looked at the computer and explained to Ted where the room was, then he pushed the button on the council, and the door opened. Ted thanked him, and the receptionist nodded. They were close to seeing Shawn.

Chapter Forty

Two days passed, and Shawn was still in his room. The family was in the room with him as Terri was exhausted. She would be leaving shortly to go home and shower. Before doing so, the doctor told the family that a family therapist would be coming in.

Ted was frustrated as he didn't like the idea of his son seeing a 'shrink.' *A therapist will come in and mess with my son as he is already dealing with issues. Damn hospital!* Ted thought while pacing a little while Terri sat on the side of the bed with Shawn and the girls were in chairs.

"Do you think this is a good idea?" Ted asked while looking at Terri.

Terri looked at him with tired eyes and answered, "I think Shawn needs to see someone, especially considering his ordeal."

Ted disagreed with Terri, but he remained supportive of his son. Shawn was sitting up, drinking orange juice, and eating eggs. Terri smiled while watching him eat his breakfast.

"Definitely, not a home-cooked meal, huh, honey?" Terri asked with a smile, and Shawn nodded in agreement. "Mom, when are you leaving? I wanna go with you," Marla asked while Lauri stayed with her father.

"When the therapist comes, I think I'll leave, perhaps afterward, doubting he or she will tell me what they think," Terri said while sitting back as Ted looked at her, seeing the exhaustion kicking in.

"Why don't you leave now and come back tonight? I'll stay." Ted offered to stay while Lauri was also staying.

Terri looked at him, and she was against leaving Shawn. A 'mother's instinct was to stick with their sick child.

"A couple more minutes, and then, we'll head out and come back tonight, ok?" She asked Ted while he glanced at her with a concerned look, and he nodded.

"Hello, I'm Dr. Reed. I'm a child therapist for the State Of Maine." Doctor Reed walked in and caught the family slightly off-guard.

Ted turned around and was the first to greet Dr. Reed.

"Hello, I'm Ted Patterson, and this is my family..." Ted did the introduction, and Dr. Reed shook hands with everyone as he looked at Shawn, and he could see something was *off*.

With your permission, I would like to speak with Shawn alone. This would require an introduction, and we'll go from there," Dr. Reed suggested while being respectful, and both Terri and Ted agreed. Ted and Terri guided their girls out of the room, but before, Terri kissed her son on the forehead while Dr. Reed watched on before sitting down and taking out a notepad from his briefcase.

Dr. Reed sat in a chair with his hair combed and garnishing light-rimmed glasses with a clean-shaven face. He wore a brown suit with a black tie and was seen as a neatly dressed doctor.

Shawn looked at his hands and saw he was not married, nor did he see any imprints indicating he was a ring bearer.

"How are you feeling this morning?" Dr. Reed asked with his notepad and a black pen with a golden tip.

Shawn sat back, finishing his breakfast, as he wasn't too interested in seeing another doctor, but..." I'm doing ok but a little tired."

"I understand that. As I said, this is an introduction, and we'll cover a couple of things and continue on another visit." Dr. Reed said that he was ready to ask another question.

"Have you had bad dreams or nightmares from your unfortunate experience?" Shawn glanced at Dr. Reed, and he initially thought of not telling Dr. Reed of the endless nightmares that haunted him, but he was a little worried that his parents might get into trouble as well. *I don't want Mom and Dad to get into trouble if I tell Dr. Reed about my nightmares.* A look of concern was shown on Shawn's face as he was afraid that somehow Dr. Reed would place blame on his parents.

"Will Mom and Dad get into trouble answering these questions, Dr. Reed?" Shawn asked, reached over, and took a sip of orange juice.

Dr. Reed adjusted his glasses and looked at Shawn, seeing the boy concerned about his parents. "Shawn, nothing is going to happen to your parents. They have concerns as well as mine, which is why I'm here. What *you* went through while in the hands of that awful man is our concern," Dr. Reed said with reassurance.

Shawn looked at him with his tired and pale face and nodded.

"So, let's try this again. *Have* you had any nightmares about the situation you went through?"

Shawn glanced down at the edge of the bed. "I have nightmares every time I sleep. It's hard to sleep...I *don't* know what to do!" The frustration within Shawn's words was concerning and worrisome. Dr. Reed wanted to tell Shawn that everything would be ok, but he couldn't make any promises.

"These nightmares happen every time you sleep, you said?" Dr. Reed wanted to make sure he had the correct info.

"Yes, every time!" Shawn said while taking another sip of his orange juice, which was now almost gone, and all he had was water with the cubes mostly melted.

"What are the nightmares about, Shawn?"

Shawn didn't immediately respond, which was a little disturbing.

"Can we talk about something else?" Shawn asked while his eyes gazed at Dr. Reed with innocence.

"Sure, let's move on, and we'll focus our efforts on something else for the time being," Dr. Reed said, and they moved on.

Chapter Forty-One

Det. Mitchell arrived at the rest area with three state cruisers. He got out of his car, as they got their firearms ready, and immediately made sure the rest area was closed to ensure no one could leave or arrive.

The rest area was searched at first, and then Det. Mitchell took them up to the old house, where he found the dead bodies and the killer.

"Troopers…I want to check every square inch of this house. To see if the suspect had been here since I was here," he said with a firm tone.

Det. Mitchell hoped the bodies were still there, but identifying these victims will be challenging. *I want to know if these bodies are related to the missing persons listed.* He thought while he and the crew were at the old house, they were walking through some rough brush, and CSI was on standby until the word had been given. Det. Mitchell wanted to be careful, but then…the house was in sight.

Det. Mitchell had his firearm out as he and his squad slowly made their way onto the property. Det. Mitchell rushed to the front of the house while stepping on dead leaves and scraps of paint that had been peeled due to weather exposure.

He waved his hand to the squad that it was okay to come as the truck he had seen the first was not in the driveway.

To his surprise, Capt. Morse showed up without his acknowledgment, and she walked up to him as the squad broke through the front door and the bodies were discovered.

The acrid smell of dead bodies filled the air in the house and made it seem unbearable to be in. Det. Mitchell knew the smell well too often from his previous visit. Capt. Morse covered her mouth with a mask as she came prepared as she and Det. Mitchell searched the house and Det. Mitchell showed her where he hid when the killer came home.

"Wow! You hid in a closet while holding a firearm?" She smirked at him.

Det. Mitchell smiled back at her and said, "I know. I didn't know if the killer had a weapon of some sort," he suggested while the squad called in CSI, and they were on their way to the old house.

"I can't believe you found this place!" Capt. Morse said while her eyes glanced around, and Det. Mitchell nodded.

"My gut instance told me to go further. I knew we were close to something but didn't know how close."

"So, the killer lived here while he walked through the woods and was making his killings at the rest area, and this was his quick getaway. Do we know if this house has an actual owner?" Capt. Morse asked while looking at Det. Mitchell.

"I'm glad you asked that question. I'm running a background check and just waiting for the results," He said while they continued to walk.

Capt. Morse and Det. Mitchell back into the other room where the bodies were, and Capt. Morse held her mask tight to her face as the smell grew worse.

Alright, I need to go outside," she said while needing a little air and Det. Mitchell complied with her.

"Whooo, that was a lot!"

"I agree, but I think either of those victims is associated with the missing person report. Maybe we should keep a lookout and see if this killer will return," Det. Mitchell and Capt. Morse agreed.

I do have one question, though. Do *you* know where that road goes to?" Capt. Morse pointed to the driveway and Det. Mitchell glanced at the driveway and dirt road.

"That's a good question. We *need* to see where it goes." Det. Mitchell decided to walk it while hinting at Capt. Morse to join him.

At first, there was reluctance, and then, she joined him as they walked the dirt road to find out where it went.

Chapter Forty-Two

Shawn had slept for about six hours last night, and the nurses were check-ing his vital signs, and he was irritated by them. They would wake him up at midnight to see if he was all right or if he needed anything like something to drink or snack on, but he just wanted to sleep.

I'm so tired. I wish they would let me sleep; that way, I would feel better. I want to go home and be in my room and play with my toys, but I've never seen my new home, only my old one.

Shawn thought as he was a little depressed. His eyes gazed out through his hospital window as the cold air smothered the corners of his widow.

Staff came in as they were doing more vitals almost every hour, and Shawn glanced at the nurse; sometimes, it was different, and he asked one of them, "Why am I getting checked on a lot?"

"We want to make sure you're gonna be okay to go home," a nurse with sharp-curved eyes showcased a hairy mole on her left lip said while Shawn's eyes were baggy and his face was pale.

It seemed now that he was in a medical prison where he was woken a lot, almost by the hour, and was nearly driven mad by the endless night visits.

The TV was playing an animated X-MEN show, and Shawn watched it to calm his nerves. He wanted to lash out at the staff or run and hide and sneak out of the hospital. In honesty, he understood why he was in the hospital, the interviews, and the nightly visits from different nurses. He understood that a madman had kidnaped him, but he just wanted to go home, his *new* home, and spend time with his family.

He wiped his eyes from tears and refocused on the TV show, which featured his favorite: MAGNETO. He smiled as he watched his favorite character lift Wolverine like a metal chandelier and toss him into a wall.

The nurse with the curved eyes had told him her name before, but he had lost track. They all looked the same to him, except for their faces and the smell of their breath.

He had seen six nurses, each with their style or *way. Two like to smoke. One likes to chew gum. The others are coffee drinkers, as I can smell the Irish cream on their breath.* He thought while the nurse with the curved eyes stared at the TV while taking his vitals.

Shawn's family had gone home for the night as they were exhausted, and Terri was returning to work in a couple, knowing that Shawn was now out of the 'red zone.' It meant he was no longer in danger, and his body improved.

"Is there anything I can get for you?" The nurse asked after checking his vitals and ensuring his IV flowed nicely.

"I'm fine. Thank you," he said with a frustrated tone.

The nurse nodded and walked out of the room. Shawn laid back on his back and watched TV, then fell asleep while watching TV.

During the night, nurses walked by as Shawn's eyes were closed, and he was sleeping peacefully. At one point, his nurse came in and saw he was sleeping peacefully, so she decided to leave him alone. A smile was groomed on her face, seeing that Shawn was doing well.

Chapter Forty-Three

Det. Mitchell was asleep in his chair while at work as there were pictures of the victims. He received a text from his daughter that she was staying at a friend's house. Det. Mitchell was relieved as he felt terrible for leaving her alone, but *she was safe, and I appreciated her letting me know.* He thought while reading the text earlier, and then, hours later, his eyes were closed.

It was 10 pm. Det. Mitchell got the call he was waiting for.

Det. Mitchell almost fell over in his chair, answered his work phone, and picked it up.

"Det. Mitchell?" The voice said softly over the phone.

"This is. Who's this?" He asked firmly.

"My name is Eric Rollins, and I am part of the CSI team. I was there. I didn't meet you. Of all nights, I decided to work late tonight. I guess I'm not the only one." Eric said while he started to give Det. Mitchell, any results?

"Please tell me you have something for me, Eric?!" Det. Mitchell asked, almost pleading.

"Yes, sir. We found a single fingerprint on the doorknob that leads into one of the bedrooms, and the fingerprint is not yours or anyone else; except, perhaps the suspect's," Eric said with a confident tone and explained to Det. Mitchell that the person showed no records, but he was confident enough that it was the suspect's

"Nice job, Eric!" Det. Mitchell said ecstatically, and he knew he would be able to find something.

"Is there a way to find out whose fingerprint that is? I know we use records, but I'm curious."

"It depends on the fingerprint. If this person's fingerprint had been scanned beforehand, it would take a little longer, sir."

"Thanks again, Eric! Nice job!" Det. Mitchell said.

"Thank you, sir, and you're welcome," Eric said. He told Det. Mitchell said he would try to dig deeper, but it was slightly doubtful.

I understand. Thanks again, Eric!"

"You're welcome, sir."

Det. Mitchell hung the phone up and looked at his computer, but before returning to work, he needed more coffee.

Det. Mitchell paced a little, thinking and waiting for his coffee to brew. He started thinking about what he could use or look for. *Something* that he was missing, and then, he remembered asking Capt. Morse about the house and who was or is the owner.

After stirring cream into his coffee, he returned to his desk and sat down. He hadn't checked his emails in a while, and Capt. Morse told him she would look into the house.

He logged into the Maine State Police internal email system. He took sips of his coffee while searching through endless emails. There were job postings, spam emails, and emails about the Maine State Trooper newsletter.

Suddenly, he found it! There was an email from Capt. Morse came in two hours ago. He eagerly opened it and read it.

It read as:

Hi Paul,

I saw that you were yawning at your desk when I left. I'm going to bed after sending this to you. So, a real estate agent named Matt Kearns emailed me about properties in that area where the old house is, and he told me Sonya, and Hugh Anderson owned it. After this, I looked at both of the records, and Sonya had nothing, but then, I looked at Hugh, and sure enough, he was shot and killed at a small rest area in Augusta. He'd been involved in some stuff related to a murder in Dexter, and witnesses pointed him out. It's getting weirder after this. Sonya was home, but they had a son, and he was in the car with his father when Hugh refused to get out of the car and threatened to kill his son. A State trooper saw a gun, and shots were fired, according to the police records. The son's name was Ted Anderson. After suffering from the trauma, Ted was taken to AMHI in Augusta, where he was evaluated and released. Afterward, Sonya took her son, Ted, and they moved out of state. The home was never sold. According to more digging by yours truly, Sonja changed her son's last name to her maiden name, Patterson. Also, Hugh's nickname was 'Duke.' According to reports and interviews, he walked a little like John Wayne, and was given that nickname along with his accent; which had a southern accent, but I couldn't find any more info on his childhood. I was unable to find anything more about Sonja. This isn't much, but I hope this helps. Get some sleep, Detective.

-Capt. Morse.

Det. Mitchell stared at the computer after reading the email and was dumbfounded. He looked at the clock on his computer, which said 10:32 PM. He knew he had to make some calls.

He emailed Capt. Morse and thanked her. He saw attachments sent from her, which he almost didn't see. *I'm no expert when it comes to computers.* He thought while opening the attachments that Capt. Morse had sent him.

There was the report of the shootout of Hugh Anderson.

The report indicated that Hugh Anderson was shot seven times while his son, Ted Anderson, watched. He was not harmed but suffered 'psycho-social effects.' He read that Ted was taken to AMHI in Augusta and was treated for several days for the extreme trauma that he was affected by the shootout and seeing his father die harshly.

Det. Mitchell read that Hugh was involved in two murders of teenagers and two robberies. A *high-speed chase led to the small rest area, and he pulled a gun, pointed it at the police, and opened fire.*

He was shot seven times. One shot to the head and the rest to the body as he bled dreadfully. Locals were happy and felt safe. The killer was dead! Det. Mitchell read, and then, he lied back in his chair, and he thought, *how can a killer be dead for almost 25 years and all suddenly show up?* Det. Mitchell kept thinking, and suddenly he realized, *copycat?*

Det. Mitchell was astonished *at how someone could have their child with them during this awful situation.* He thought while briefly leaning over, picking up his coffee, and taking sips.

He held his coffee while looking at the reports and trying to place some things together. *What effects would that have on a child, and how would they exist today?* His eyes glazed at the attachment, and he wished he could gain medical records, but he knew there would be a lot of hurdles.

He stood up and started to pace, and then, it came to him. "Is it possible that Ted Patterson, Shawn's father is the same person who was Ted Anderson?" He asked out loud to himself while no one was around.

"How could I proceed with this?"

He looked at the clock on the computer, which said 11:00 PM, and decided to visit Shawn, but it would be risky as Shawn's parents might not be there. *I have to do the homework, but I know I could be in trouble without one of Shawn's parents, but I need to know if Shawn knows anything about his father.* Det. Mitchell thought while grabbing his coat and leaving for the hospital.

Chapter Forty-Four

Terri stirred in her sleep as she felt Ted getting up from bed; she woke up and could see him gripping his head and griping in pain as she knew he was dealing with another headache.

Terri slowly got up and sat on the edge of the bed while Ted walked down the stairwell. The hardwood floor was cold, so she put on her slippers and robe. She walked out of the bedroom while hearing Ted down below, stirring and moaning, as she knew he was echoing his pain.

"Honey, are you ok?" She asked while her right hand was on the rail as she walked down the stairs. There was no answer, and she continued to make her way.

Her robe drifted lightly as most of it was made of silk; she walked into the living room as Ted would take pain meds and lie down afterward, hoping to sleep off his headache.

The living room was dim, except for the kitchen night light above the stove. She walked around to the couch and could see his legs hanging over the edge of the couch. She decided not to turn on the lights, knowing it would hurt Ted's eyes.

She walked around and sat on the edge of the couch, she could see his body, but his face was hidden. "Honey, are you ok?" She asked with a concerned tone, and there was no response.

She reached out with gentleness, and she touched his thigh.

He moaned a little, and then, he reached and touched her hand.

"Honey, your hand is *cold*. Are you ok?" She asked again while she was surprised by the sudden coldness of his hands. Beforehand, his hands were always warm due to his blood pressure.

There was no verbal response, but only his gentle coldness touched her, and then, his hand started to go towards her vaginal area.

"Alright, not now!" She joked, and then, she felt something was *off.* "Ted?" She asked with a nervous tone, and then, his hand tried to reach her vaginal area again, and she pushed it away, but there was a 'roughness.'

"TED! STOP IT!" She yelled, and then, he spoke. "Ted is not here anymore, honeybee…*Only* Duke…" Terri screamed, and she tried to fight off his sudden aggression, but he was too strong. Terri screamed, and she saw Duke get up and grip her mouth with his sudden strength, and there was a nasty odor attached to him. She started to push away, and Duke gripped her tightly.

Duke's southern accent was raspy and filled with rage. "GET AWAY FROM ME!" She was able to get away after pushing him off.

She fell to the floor with a sudden *THUMP!* "Now, honeybee…no need to be that way! Dukie boy *will* make you a real woman!" He said while she could hear the sudden heaviness of his feet.

"TED! TED! TED, HELP ME!" She yelled for him, and there was no answer.

"I told you, bitch…Teddy is gone!" She cried as Duke followed her with a slight rusty laugh. The smell in the room grew acrid, and Terri screamed; suddenly, her daughters were awake and were on the stairway.

"MOM, ARE YOU OK?" Lauri asked while Duke stood still, and Terri yelled. "GET OUT!" The girls screamed, and Duke walked over to Terri, and he reached down and gripped her hair with a sudden tightness, pulling and starting to choke her.

"DIE BITCH! When I'm done with you, your girly girls will be next…." His voice was raspy and nasty.

"YOU'RE NOT GONNA HURT MY BABIES!" Terri yelled as she tried to bite Duke's hand, but it was not working. Suddenly, Duke was forced to let go and fell onto the couch.

Terri layed face first, with his tears falling onto the cold floor.

Terri slowly got up, and she could hear moaning from the other side of the couch. It had tipped over, with Duke landing on it with a thrust.

"Terri, GET THE GIRLS OUTTA HERE!" Ted yelled, and Terri stood up and asked, "TED, COME WITH ME!"

"I CAN'T! GET THEM OUT!" Ted shouted as there was some physical struggle behind the couch, but she could not see what was happening.

Voices of Ted and Duke echoed ferociously as they were arguing and fighting.

"I LOVE YOU, TED!" Terri said, and Duke replied, "I'll be coming soon for you, BITCH!"

"I LOVE YOU, TERRI!" Ted responded, and the struggle continued, but she suddenly heard the front window smashing and yelled for Ted.

"TED!?" Terri reached the top of the stairwell and called for the girls. They exited Lauri's room, and Lauri ensured she and Marla were safe. Terri decided to go out the window as another level would be a stepping stone for them. Terri slowly guided them, one by one, as she kept looking behind her, but she saw that Ted's vehicle was leaving.

Terri and the girls escaped, while Duke and Ted were nowhere in sight.

Chapter-Forty-Five

Det. Mitchell arrived at the hospital, hoping to see Shawn, but he knew he was breaking some rules as he would be interviewing a minor. He started to walk around the nurses' station, and Shawn was just down the hallway.

"Hello, detective? Can I help you?" The head nurse asked while recognizing and having seen him come in before to speak with Shawn and his family.

I'm here to see Shawn Patterson, please?" Deep down, he pleaded a little, knowing he could not see a minor without their parent's permission.

"Detective, I cannot allow you to see him. For one thing, he's sleeping, and two, neither of the parents is here at this time of night. Please come back when they're here," she said with a kind tone, but Det. Mitchell knew he would also do some pleading, maybe a little begging.

"I understand that, but this is an open case, and Shawn is a witness! I'm sure you understand what's going on since it's been all over the news and stuff," Det. Mitchell reiterated, and the head nurse looked at him sternly as her patience had worn thin.

"Det. Mitchell, either leave, or I'm calling security!" Her voice was raised, and some of the staff heard her.

"No need to raise your tone, Ma'am." Det. Mitchell said with a slight smile.

"What's going on here?" A voice from the head nurse was heard, and it was Dr. Reed.

"Det. Mitchell is requesting to see the boy without his parents' permission, and he is arguing with me," she said while Dr. Reed walked up next to her and nodded.

"Understood. Detective, please follow me to my office," Dr. Reed said softly, and Det. Mitchell nodded and followed while the head nurse watched.

"As you know, seeing a minor without their parent's consent is a big 'No-no' and could result in your termination of employment if your superiors were able to find out," Dr. Reed said while he and Det. Mitchell were walking down a hallway filled with patients and beds. They walked past two sets of double doors, and they were near Dr. Reed's office. "Well, this is an interesting wing," Det. Mitchell said while his eyes gazed at the rooms, filled with screaming patients while others were sitting still on their beds and staring at the wall with lifeless eyes.

"These patients are the ones that go beyond the medical field…they need more of the psychological approach if you get what I'm saying, Detective," Dr. Reed said while making a turn, and Det. Mitchell felt a slight uneasiness.

Dr. Reed opened a door with his name in a gold bracket with a black background and gold trim.

"Please sit down, Detective," Dr. Reed insisted, pointing to a chair across from Dr. Reed's desk.

They both sat down while Det. Mitchell gazed at numerous photos, and then, something caught his eye. He got up and walked over to a medium-sized framed photo, a picture of the old AMHI hospital.

Standing in the foreground with the nursing staff and other doctors was a young doctor with combed hair and black-rimmed glasses.

Is this you?" Det. Mitchell pointed, asking Dr. Reed, who nodded and said, "Yes, Detective, that's me. My name is listed in the column just below it.

"Well, how old are you there?"

"I was twenty-eight, and it was my first year there. Now, can we talk about Shawn Patterson?" Dr. Reed asked with an insistent tone.

Det. Mitchell walked back to the chair and sat down while seeing endless rewards and degrees of Dr. Reed.

"I hoped to interview Shawn Patterson again as I found something out."

"What did you find out, Detective?" Dr. Reed asked, his eyes glaring at Det. Mitchell was slightly uneasy as he didn't care for the office, and *there was something creepy about this guy as he was staring at me.* Det. Mitchell thought while answering Dr. Reed's question.

"Well, you know I can't discuss an ongoing investigation, doctor. I just need to see him."

"Why this sudden urgency with tonight? His parents will be back tomorrow morning and are his legal guardians, but he *is* under my care. I hope you understand that, detective," Dr. Reed asked with steely eyes. Det. Mitchell was slightly agitated, but then, "I understand that, doctor. It concerns his father, Ted Patterson. I found out he was at AMHI as a child after his father was killed in a shootout, but I dunno what happened after that," Det. Mitchell explained as Dr. Reed sat back in his chair and listened to Det. Mitchell explain.

"Do you know anything about why he was there? I mean, wasn't that place for the insane or somethin'?" Det. Mitchell was unsure why children were sent there.

"Detective, I was there! As you know from the photo and from what I told you. And yes, Mr. Patterson was under my care. He was there for many weeks, not days. The trauma of seeing his father shot dead by the state police was devasting, and the mother agreed to place him there."

"So, what happened?" Det. Mitchell asked, hoping that Dr. Reed would give him some clues.

"Ted was distressed upon entering that facility, but it would take more than days to accompany him and his issues. He would talk about his father and how much he hated the state police. Now, Detective, I don't have to tell you anything since it pertains to patient confidelity. Do you understand?" Dr. Reed said with an egotistical tone.

"I understand, Dr. Reed. But, also, I am dealing with an open case that seems to be connected, but I don't think Ted would kidnap his son and keep him locked up for months…that would be unheard of!"

"Detective, it wasn't Ted that did that…it was his father, Duke."

A heaviness grew on his face as Dr. Reed examined his reaction and Det. Mitchell asked the following question. "What do you mean his *father*…Duke, did?"

Dr. Reed stood up while his chair sprung forward a little, and he walked around his desk and was going to escort Det. Mitchell.

"I wish I could tell you…."

"Dr. Reed…I NEED TO KNOW!" Det. Mitchell asked urgently, and Dr. Reed placed his hand on Det. Mitchell's shoulder…."I can't tell you!" He uttered.

"His father is dead! He couldn't survive that ordeal, doctor…please tell me!" Det. Mitchell pleaded with him, and Dr. Reed stopped with a great reluctance at first, then proceeded to tell him.

Chapter Forty-Six

Shawn was asleep when his room grew darker, with *someone* dimming the lighting in the room. The door closed without a sound as Shawn was sleeping soundly. The TV lighting lit the room as the blankets on Shawn were slowly removed.

A hand started reaching Shawn with abnormal veins and a skull ring on the index finger. "Hello, sunshine…time to wake up and go for a ride…." The stranger's voice said in a hushed tone, and then, the door opened, and it was the head nurse.

The stranger quickly went to the side, hiding in the corner of the room as the nurse didn't see him.

"Already, just checking on your vitals…" she said with a whisper while trying to be quiet.

A slight nervousness grew within her as she felt *someone* else in the room, and then, she finished up.

She turned quickly and was met with a man who revealed his face to her, and she started to scream, but he gripped her jaw and squeezed.

She struggled as he lifted her off the floor with great strength and tried fighting, but he continued crushing her jaw, and she fell. Her body quivered as blood rivered from her mouth, and her eyes were wide open.

He walked over the dead nurse and over to Shawn, who was still asleep. "Boy, must have given some kind of sleeping shit….either way, we're going for a ride, Shawnie boy," the stranger said while picking up Shawn and carrying him.

He ensured Shawn was warm by wrapping him up in a blanket, and the stranger carried Shawn as his eyes peeked out of the room, and there was no one around. He quickly glanced while Shawn remained asleep and unaware.

The stranger walked swiftly while trying to avoid anyone, but as he left, a nurse came around the corner and yelled, "HEY!?" The stranger quickly turned to her and yelled, "FUCK YOU!" Her face suddenly filled with fear, and she was stunned by what she saw.

The stranger quickly jogged with Shawn in his arms, and the nurse ran over to the nurse's desk and hit the alarm. The stranger had planned this and parked his truck closer.

After hitting each button with his foot, he used the head nurse's key card, which he took after killing her, and then used it to open the exit door and kicked it open with great force.

"Time to go home, boy!" The stranger said while jogging to his truck, and he opened it and placed Shawn in the front, and he ran to the other side, turned the truck on, and quickly drove off. While driving, he put the seatbelt on Shawn as Shawn stirred a little.

"What's….What's happening…?" He murmured.

"Don't worry about it, boy…Duke The Man got you!" Duke said with a rough tone, and he drove out of the hospital parking lot while security ran out with one officer who had a coffee spill on his uniform after the alarm was pushed.

Duke and Shawn got away…

Chapter-Forty-Seven

Minutes Before…

Dr. Reed guided Det. Mitchell to his office and wanted to explain to him, now that he had revealed some of what had happened to Ted, but there was more.

"So, you're saying she is a little crazy or somethin'?" Det. Mitchell said with a disbelief tone.

"No, what I am saying…."

Dr. Reed stopped as he looked at Det. Mitchell, who looked at him with disbelief and waited for his explanation.

"Mr. Patterson *has another personality and* revealed himself to be called 'Duke.' Det. Mitchell's look grew more serious, and he asked, "What are you saying, doctor…this *Duke* personality killed and kidnapped his son?"

"That's the point, Detective…Duke is *not* Ted or vice versa…they know each other, but when Duke decided to come out after of these years, but I don't know why…." Dr. Reed said with a disappointed tone.

"Alight, Doctor…So, why would he keep Ted's son alive and not kill him?" Det. Mitchell asked with a serious tone.

Dr. Reed glanced at him and said, "I think Ted somehow told him not to kill his son, but there is *something* more you need to know, Det. Mitchell…"

"What!?"

"When Duke came through, he just didn't come through; he physically changed…*changed* to something more ugly than his father, he physically changed from having no tattoo to having them. His tone changed, and everything about him did!"

Det. Mitchell looked at Dr. Reed and had heard that a personality could physically change when multiple personalities had come through.

167

"Well, either way…that son of bitch will be gettin' a bullet between those crooked eyes!" Det. Mitchell said, and the alarm went off, and Dr. Reed looked at the glowing red light and said, "He's here…."

Det. Mitchell ran out of the office to Shawn's room, which was on the other side as he told security to lock all doors. He took out his cell and called Terri.

"Terri!?" She answered.

"Hello?"

"Where's your husband?"

"I dunno. Why?"

"Shawn's gone!" Paul said with a rushed tone as he reached Shawn's room and saw the dead nurse on the floor.

"WHAT DO YOU MEAN?!" She asked while he could hear her gathering her stuff and waking the girls up.

"DUKE'S GOT HIM!"

"I'M ON MY WAY!" She yelled.

"NO! MEET ME AT THE REST AREA, AND I'LL TELL YOU MORE!" He yelled and then hung up the phone while Terri was getting the girls up and leaving.

Det. Mitchell looked at the dead nurse while staff examined her and Det. Mitchell called Capt. Morse and told her what happened.

"I'll get all available units over there immediately!" She said as they hung up.

Det. Mitchell rushed out of the hospital and was on his way to the rest area.

Chapter-Forty-Eight

Rest Area

Duke had Shawn with him at the Augusta Rest Area and sat in the truck, staring at the lights and people coming and going.

"I wanna go home!" Shawn said, still feeling fuzzy after the hospital had given him meds to relax him.

Duke's physical features were far different than those of Ted, Shawn's father. His eyes were black, his face rough, and his cheekbones were small boulders. In the rearview mirror, lights flashed as the state, county, and local police arrived and surrounded Duke and Shawn.

Shawn rubbed his eyes as the lights were almost blinding. The sun appeared from the corners of the clouds, revealing more features of Duke to Shawn. His eyes gazed at him, not seeing his father anymore as he saw that his father was still there based on his drive.

"Dad, is that you?" Shawn asked with an innocent tone.

"Sorry, Shawnie-boy…Daddy's gone!" Duke said while his eyes looked around and glared at the police. He saw that Det. Mitchell arrived, and just behind him were Terri and the girls.

"MOM!" Shawn shouted as he saw his mother and sisters.

"Please let me go…." He pleaded as it seemed to upset Duke a little more, and Duke responded, "SHUT UP!" He yelled and turned to Shawn, who was scared and huddled within the side of the passenger door as it was locked.

"Please let me go…" he pleaded again, and Duke yelled at him, "SHUT THE FUCK UP!" Shawn shimmered slightly as Duke's tone was rough and rugged.

Lights glared onto the truck's windshield as Duke stared at the lights, as he was in a trance, and then, he reached down while suddenly staring at Det. Mitchell pulled out a .44. Shawn's eyes lit up, and started to cry.

Det. Mitchell and other officers had their firearms out, and Duke took out the 44. He turned to look at Shawn, who was crying, and Duke smiled as he enjoyed seeing the young boy crying and in pain. Shawn saw his mother and wanted to yell out, but he was afraid to as Duke had yelled at him. Now, Duke has a firearm. Shawn looked up at Duke and said, "Please don't kill me…I___don't wanna die!" he pleaded, and Duke smirked, pulled on the trigger, and pointed at Shawn.

"Shawnie-Boy…this is for your good, son." Duke said, and then Shawn looked at him and said with tears running down his cheeks, "Daddy, I love you…."

Duke's arm struggled as the firearm wiggled in front of Shawn's face, and then, he retracted the weapon and slowly pointed it up at his face, but there was an internal struggle as Shawn watched in horror.

"SHAWN, DO IT!" His father's voice came through, and Shawn quickly leaned forward and pulled the trigger. Duke's face exploded as flesh and blood filled the driver's side while Shawn screamed and held his ears.

The driver's side window had shattered as Det. Mitchell got a tire wrench from his car and smashed the window, as blood covered the rest of the seats and landed on Shawn's lap.

Det. Mitchell reached in and unlocked the door. A trooper from Shawn's side opened the door and grabbed Shawn. Shawn held his ears as they were hurting from the loudness of the firearm within the truck.

Det. Mitchell opened the driver's side door, and Duke's body spilled out with pieces of brains and blood covering the ground. His body quivered once as Det. Mitchell held his firearm to Duke, who was dead! Shawn had some blood on him, but most of the mess went on the rest of the seat.

The trooper and Shawn embraced quickly as the trooper rushed Shawn away from the truck, and Shawn brought him to Terri and the girls. Det. Mitchell stared at Duke, who was astonished at the physical transformation. *I had met this guy, who was Ted, but now…I see a different guy, and his name was Duke…*Det. Mitchell thought in disbelief and walked away from the truck as the paramedics rushed over.

Capt. Morse stood by the line of officers. Paul looked at her and nodded. She placed her hand on his shoulder as Det. Mitchell walked past her, and Capt. Morse took over the scene.

Chapter-Forty-Nine

The Last Chapter

Weeks passed since the passing of Ted/Duke, and Shawn sat in the leathered-covered chair while Terri was with him, and Dr. Reed saw him.

"How are you doing, Shawn?" Dr. Reed asked while the visits were placed at Maine General Hospital. Shawn's eyes were lifeless, and he had not spoken a word since the incident.

"Will he ever talk again?' Terri asked with a concerned tone.

"Yes, he will. It's just a matter of time, Mrs. Patterson."

While watching her son, Terri sat mute while dealing with the loss of her husband, whom she never knew had gone through so much. *I wish ted had told me….I miss him so much!* She thought while starting to cry.

"Here you go, Mrs. Patterson," Dr. Reed said while handing her a tissue and asking what happened to Ted to bring out Duke.

"Based on previous reports, he fell and hit his head before moving; is that correct?"

"Yes, that's correct."

"Between that and some stress may have caused Duke to come out, but I think Duke was tired of being suppressed all those years, and it just happened!" He explained while he looked at Shawn, who was looking down at the floor.

"What will happen to Shawn?" Terri asked while wiping her tears with the tissues given to her.

"It's going to take time, but I think with time, medications, and some therapy, I think he'll come around," Dr. Reed said while looking at Shawn.

He wrote notes in his yellow notebook.

"How are you holding up?" he asked while turning to her.

"I can't believe my husband is dead! He was the father of my children, and now, he's gone!" More tears came down her pale cheeks as the stress had been overbearing for her.

"I do have a couple of questions, though. I think this one the police will want. How did Mr. Patterson get the truck and have the license plate made to say, DUKE1?" Dr. Reed asked with a curious tone.

"I know he bought it with the truck, but I'm not sure about the nameplate," Terri said while glancing at Shawn.

"Why didn't he keep Shawn in that old house that the police found instead of that old shack?" Terri asked Dr. Reed, who looked at his notes and then back at her.

"Honestly, I'm not sure. Based on the police reports published by various news sources, the old house had bodies in it, and it was just... disturbing," Dr. Reed said while not knowing Shawn was kept in a shack and not in the house.

"I'm sorry this happened, though; the conclusion was less than positive. I wish I could do more...Ted was deeply troubled as a child, and I did my best to help him. I'm confident that Duke will be a distant memory." Dr. Reed smiled, assuring Terri that Shawn would recover while Shawn lifted his head and slowly smiled...

The End...

Works By Duane E. Coffill

1. Nightbeast
2. The Path
3. Cursed Darkness
4. The Eyes Within
5. Dark Voices
6. The Well.

Duane also has a story in the anthology "Northern Frights" by the Horror Writers Of Maine called "Window Of Darkness."

You can find Duane on Instagram, Twitter, and Facebook. For more info, please visit his website: www.horrorwriterduanecoffill.com

www.ingramcontent.com/pod-product-compliance
Lightning Source LLC
Chambersburg PA
CBHW072134300726
48975CB00003B/1058